I0623579

TERRIBLE
KARISMA

An
Unfortunate
Lineage

Volume
I

A Novella

Also Available
by **Delaine Christine** through
Kimerah Publishing

AN UNFORTUNATE LINEAGE
Terrible Karisma – I
Kayos Effect – II
Karisma Trouble – III
Total Kayos – IV
Deadly Karisma – V
Kayos Knows – VI

Karisma Kayos: Out of Time
Vol VII (Finale)

TERRIBLE

KARISMA

An
Unfortunate
Lineage

Volume
I

A Novella

Delaine Christine

Terrible Karisma
An Unfortunate Lineage Volume I

ISBN-13: 978-1950563012

Book and Cover Design by DC Johnson
Model Pic by Lindsey Soard Photography, used with permission
Road Cover Image by Vitaly Kriyosheev
Interior Model Image by Badmanproduction, used with permission

Kimerah Publishing, Elkhart, IN

Printed in the United States of America

Dedication

To V.B.

Many thanks for opening my eyes.

-K.K.

The Prophecy

A prophecy was made this day
a healing path is on the way.

Two of mirror image there will be
crossing their paths in time you'll see...

PROLOGUE

Loveland, Colorado
Somewhere Out of Time

I struggled to sit up.

Managing to find my seat, I cradled the right side of my face where their fist had impacted. My heart thundered in my chest and my head spun.

I'd been brought to the mossy forest floor near the forked path with one very effective punch, having been taken by surprise. This both infuriated and scared the crap out of me.

Regaining my senses long enough to call out a warning, they disappeared seconds later with barely a backward glance. Taking a deep breath and a moment to think, I could feel a surge of fury rising within me. My proposal would have benefited both of us, but instead of meeting me halfway they scorned not only my offer, but me.

I rose on unsteady feet, understanding fully their anger. I had uncovered all their secrets, wholly by accident, but that part didn't seem to matter to them. They were completely indifferent to my situation and had disregarded the potential advantages of my proposal for all involved.

There was no excuse for that.

They tied my hands.

So be it. I was about to tie theirs, and I had more than enough leverage to do it with.

I walked back to the house alone only to become more aggravated when I found they locked the study door, preventing me from re-entry there. Trekking around the house to the front door my frustration increased upon discovering they locked me out of the house for the night. My blood began to boil.

Noticing a light on above the garage, I made my way toward it, knowing I'd be able to regain access to the house that way. Then I'd grab the laptop from under my bed. So far I hadn't been able to re-locate the one who gave it to me, but they told me to do with the manuscripts as I saw fit.

And that was exactly what I intended to do.

The stories on the laptop which contained all the RavenCroft family's secrets were the perfect means to an end. Finding a ghostwriter to fix the manuscripts and make them look like I intended to publish them shouldn't be too difficult. I'd have to use an alias, but once they saw how far I'd go, maybe then they'd take me seriously.

Chapter 1

A Week Later

"Is this where I do my thing?"

I could hear the ghostwriter sigh through my laptop speaker.

"Yes, if you must. But I don't see why you need to do this. Most people won't like it."

"Sure they will. They're gonna *love* me!"

Ignoring her snort of laughter, I cleared my throat and decided to begin my narration by allowing my real personality to come through. Adjusting the microphone attached to the computer, I clicked on record and started to speak only to be interrupted.

"Remember to enunciate clearly. And don't forget to pause your recording between chapters. That way I know what goes where when I transcribe it."

This time I rolled my eyes. The ghostwriter I chose for this was such a nag. One would think since I was letting her list herself as the author that she'd be a little less of a pain.

"Yes, yes, I know. I'm disconnecting now."

"Just remember I need it by the end of the…"

(click) And she's gone.

Rubbing my hands together with glee, I finally begin.

- - -

Terrible.

The very definition of the word describes the nature of the story I'm about to share, and it's why I've chosen it as part of the title of this novel.

Yes, I know it says, written by Delaine Christine on the cover, but hey! I am the narrator of this tale, as well as the one who gave her this story in the first place. So there.

Who am I, you might be wondering?

I am Vortigern Black.

Or, at least, it's the name I have chosen for telling you about the RavenCrofts. It's my, for lack of a better term, narration name - sort of like an alias - for the telling of this story requires a certain amount of anonymity. Besides, I happen to think Vortigern Black is a cool name. Don't you agree?

Okay, maybe not.

Moving on.

You might be wondering why I won't tell you who I really am. It's because I'm working undercover. Deep, deep cover. So very deep, in fact, that the mere mention of my even being undercover with the assumed name puts me at risk. So, I am not going to tell you who I am, at least not yet anyway. Besides, it's a lot more fun this way. This shall be part of the allure, part of the attraction, part of the mystique, and intrigue of continuing forward in your reading. All I will tell you is that I am a character within this story. Your job, should you choose to accept it, will be to figure out who I, Vortigern Black, am as I share with you about the RavenCrofts many trials, tribulations, and the vast universal story which will eventually link them all together. We'll see at the end of their story if you've figured it out.

Incidentally, the RavenCroft name is with a capital C in it. That's not a typo. But as the supposed author of this tale points out, it makes the family I'll be telling you about that much more unusual.

She isn't kidding either. Unique doesn't even begin to describe them. But no matter how different the RavenCrofts might be they are, in the end, just as human as everyone else for they do not have fangs and they don't shape-shift or morph into different creatures or animals. They are, however, capable of things that the general population are not.

I assure you, they are not alone.

As you read, you'll soon find that this story has a little bit of everything in it. Just wait, you'll see. It has pain, it has loss, it has heartache and misery. There's a little action, intrigue, mystery, and, believe it or not, a little fantasy. How so, you ask? Because the RavenCrofts are gifted.

Gifted how, you might be wondering? And how did I, of all people, happen to come about this story?

Hhmmm.

I'll tell you this much; through a portion, or all, of this terrible tale I was there, and therefore, very much a part of it. As to their abilities … patience people. I'm getting there.

As you delve into the An Unfortunate Lineage series, there are five points to keep in mind as you read.

One, the RavenCroft family is large, comprised of six very charismatic adult children and their widowed father, Bastion RavenCroft. You'll definitely want to be paying attention in order to keep them straight.

Two, though An Unfortunate Lineage is meant to be somewhat inspirational, the three stories with Karisma in the title are a bit more secular in nature for the RavenCroft's have not grown up with the same belief system as their cousins, the Blackthorne's. That said, we don't tear off our clothes and dangle them in front of you so it's safe for the reader who might be looking for a cleaner story.

For those who truly can't stand my narration, feel free to enjoy my absence in the Kayos entitled novels.

Ms. Christine was very adamant about me not narrating those. For some reason she seemed to think you all might need a break from me.

I can't imagine why.

Three, those readers disinclined toward faith-based stories may skip the even numbered novels and move on to the Finale. That's right people. The, An Unfortunate Lineage series is what one might loosely call a "pick the plot" sort of collection. Far be it from me, or the author even, to force upon anyone matters of faith.

You should be able to still follow what's happening within the conclusion, whether you read only the Karisma stories, versus the Kayos tales, vice versa, or for that matter, you decide to skip straight to the finale. Though if you do that you will miss the fun of the conundrum that is me, Vortigern Black. Plus, there are bound to be aspects of the stories you skip that likely won't get covered in the finale, but it is entirely your call.

You have the choice.

Four, if you read the entire series you will likely find some parallels. There is a specific reason for this, which won't be explained right away. Rest assured, I will pass on what I know as I learn more.

And lastly, you need to know that this story started more than fifteen years ago with Kahner RavenCroft, the eldest of the clan, and his wife, Eliza, of only a year.

I won't lie to you; the initial part of this tale is intense.

At least, I think so.

So, grab your favorite drink, soft drink or otherwise, and a munchy or crunchy, if you haven't already, then sit back, relax and…

…enjoy!

- - -

Loveland, Colorado
One Ominous January Evening

The two figures watched the woman from a distance.

Gripping her purse with one hand, her feet crunched in the crisp snow on the ground. She walked tentatively up to the front doors of the building made up of white wooden slats and stood. Her hands trembled. Tears streaked her red swollen cheeks. She reached for the door handle only to yank it back unexpectedly as though afraid.

Fidgeting with the pendant dangling from the chain at the nape of her neck, the woman's waxen blonde head bowed submissively. Her lips – tinged with blue from the cold – moved in a silent prayer. Shoulders heaving, she cried in distress. Her watering eyes shifted towards the dark sky. Moaning softly, she cried out in despair into the star-laden night.

Fear was evident in the sounds emitting from within her and was just as prevalent in her soft amber eyes.

"Please, oh please, let it be safe to enter," she whimpered in a shaky voice.

She shivered in the cold, her winter coat not enough to dispel the overwhelming chill. Her posture was rigid and tense. Her gaze darted about as though afraid someone might be watching her.

Someone was.

From their vantage, they couldn't be seen by her or anyone else unless they wanted to be seen. Seeing the woman slowly enter the building, as though awaiting some sort of assault, they intently watched her heave a relieved sigh upon passing the threshold of the doorway.

With grim satisfaction, the two dark figures exchanged looks then followed the woman to the doorway of the building, knowing full well they could not enter. If they'd done their job right, she wouldn't be swayed.

They watched cautiously from their vantage, as she knelt and bowed her head. Clasping her hands before her, sobs wracked her body. She prayed feverishly for forgiveness for what she was about to do. What they had convinced her to do.

Another figure appeared suddenly behind her. His silver gaze was a mixture of sympathy and disappointment. At one point as she prayed, he laid a hand upon her shoulder in a consoling gesture of compassion. She simply continued praying, unaware of the presence next to her.

It wasn't time yet. She wasn't ready.

Eliza RavenCroft was too afraid. And they all knew it.

- - -

Elkhart, Texas
The Next Morning

"The lion in your future is no good for you." The elderly woman stood in the doorway of Kalysta's bedroom, leaning on a wooden cane. Her age-worn leathery features were unusually stern and she had the look of one who hastily rolled out of bed. It was barely six in the morning.

"Grams, what are you talking about?" Sitting up in bed Kalysta rubbed at her sleep filled eyes and yawned loudly.

"If cut, your life as you know it will end." There was an ominous edge to the woman's voice and her crinkling eyes appeared anxious. She pointed toward Kalysta's head with her cane, desperate for her granddaughter to pay attention.

"You mean … my hair?" The young woman fisted her hand around the length of her mocha tresses. "I'd never cut it short."

Lips pursing in agitation, she pounded her cane against the wooden floor for emphasis, imploring her granddaughter with a look to take her more seriously. "Don't let *him* cut it," she said, becoming insistent.

"Him who? Grams, you're not making any sense."

"If *he* cuts it, the choice will be made for you."

Shoving her face into her pillow Kalysta silently groaned. "Are you sure you're going to be okay on your own after I'm gone?" She was starting to have second thoughts about leaving her grandmother alone when she went off to college in the fall, but she had about eight months to reconsider if she needed to.

The old woman harrumphed indignantly. "I've been taking care of myself longer than you've been alive. You *will* go!" she croaked proudly, pointing her age worn finger at the girl now dragging herself from bed. "You study. No romance. Romance with the lion is no good for you."

"Grams, the last thing I'm looking for is romance," she assured her with a grin. "Especially with a lion. They're too shaggy and have bad breath." Planting a kiss on her grandmother's forehead, she shuffled past her toward the bathroom.

The old woman watched her go. With a heavy sigh, she fingered the two elk teeth she wore as a necklace that were nestled among the folds of her robe. "Kaly, wait," she pleaded. She pulled the leather cord over her head and hobbled over to her. Reaching over her head, she placed the cord around Kalysta's neck. "For you, for protection. Promise me you will wear it always and never let your hair be cut." She patted the Elk teeth now lying against the center of her granddaughter's chest. A sad wistful half smile played at her lips.

Kalysta took the teeth in the palm of her hand. They had been a wedding gift from a Kiowa Indian brave to her great-grandmother over a hundred years before. She hesitated.

"I thought your mother warned you not to take them off because something bad might happen if you did." She gave the woman a speculative look, wondering at what had prompted the sudden desire to pass the necklace on.

"It belongs to you now. You go away soon. The Elk spirit will go with you … keep you safe. Avoid the lion. Yes, yes, avoid the lion," she said, repeating her words as though attempting to assure them both. She silently limped away, ending the discussion. The soft thump, thump of her cane echoed down the hallway. Her hand shook as she clutched at the empty space near her heart. A single tear streaked down her cheek and worry creased her brow. She'd done what she could to keep her granddaughter safe. Now the rest was up to Kalysta.

Chapter 2

Did I tell you, or what?

Intense, right? Now, it is not my intent to pull you out of, or away from the story but there are a few things you do need to know before we continue, starting with the following.

At this point, the story picks up late afternoon, going on evening that same day near the hour of sunset. The setting is the RavenCroft family horse ranch located in a hidden valley near Loveland, Colorado. It is owned and run by, none other than, Bastion RavenCroft himself, the patriarch of the family.

At six feet five inches tall with short wavy jet-black hair and crystal-clear blue eyes, he is decidedly large and intimidating. In addition to having a slightly dark and, at times, even brooding appearance, the man is also gifted with what he believes to be the ability to have visions of future events. He also often knows things at times without knowing how or why.

Seriously, for a man to look like he does, one might argue that it's unfair for him to be blessed with such decidedly advantageous abilities. This, unfortunately, does not mean he always has a direct line to see and know when life is about to go awry. As is the case at this point in my tale, for his eldest and only married son, Kahner, is about to have a terrible, and I mean absolutely terrible day.

- - -

Kahner RavenCroft fidgeted with agitation. He sat in a plush chair in front of the fireplace in the living room as heat poured from the fire burning in the hearth. It was the middle of winter and the bitter cold that had descended upon the RavenCroft Horse Ranch left even those in the main house struggling to stay warm in those few rooms without a fireplace. Gazing toward the hearth, Kahner's thoughts shifted momentarily. He found himself grateful to his father, Bastion RavenCroft, for having the foresight to build a fireplace in nearly every room of the vast ranch house.

Eyes shifting from the flames licking at the wood to the picture windows near the front of the house, he noted lights near the driveway. He suspected one of his brothers had arrived home.

But which one?

Pulling his large frame from the chair Kahner stood, staring out the window anxiously trying to see who it was beyond the snow-covered shrubbery and foliage along the walkway. Thick snowflakes fell from the sky, dusting the patio deck and walkway, where it had been shoveled earlier in the day. A figure exited from what appeared to be a patrol car and began walking slowly towards the front of the house, leaving footprints behind in the snow. Booted feet thumped across the deck heading for the front door, but then the sound stopped. No further movement could be heard.

"What's he waiting for?" Kahner queried his father in irritation.

Worry lines were etched in Kahner's chiseled features. He ran his fingers through his short black hair and glanced again toward the solid maple wood door. Kahner attempted to glean the man's thoughts on the other side but he was too far away with a barrier between them.

"Sit down, Kahn, I'll go see what's up," Bastion ordered, coming up out of his chair near the kitchen.

His attention was grabbed by the shortened nickname, rarely used by his father. Kahner stopped abruptly in front of the fireplace, turning toward him.

They locked gazes.

His son's matching blue eyes stared back at Bastion. They were filled with fear.

At six feet five Kahner mirrored his father in height, but his build was slightly larger, broader. His muscles flexed under his shirt near his neck. Running his hands across his face in agitation he then stretched, attempting to dispel the tension from his shoulders.

"Why is he just standing there? And where did Eliza go?"

Bastion sighed. "I don't know, Kahner." He had a bad suspicion he knew the answers to both questions. His son and daughter-in-law, Eliza, had been having heated arguments all weekend long. They'd learned she was pregnant on Friday.

His son was excited.

Eliza had been terrified.

And Bastion had known why.

The abilities she was presenting with were frightening her.

The moment Eliza walked into the kitchen on Friday morning, she'd become dizzy, nearly falling to the floor, and began hearing what she described as voices in her head. When she relayed what the "voices" were saying they realized she must be pregnant, for it was the only way she could have developed Kahner's ability to know another person's thoughts. It was why his son had made a run for the pregnancy test to confirm their suspicions, for all the RavenCroft children and their father, were gifted with what they believed to be special powers.

Kahner paced in agitation as his father moved toward the front door. "How did I, of all people, not see this coming?"

"You had no warning whatsoever?" Bastion queried, his brow lifting in question. Pausing near the door he peered back at him. Eliza had disappeared the evening before after dinner and hadn't returned till late into the night. When Bastion found her on the living room couch that morning, she took off without saying a word.

"I could tell something was wrong," Kahner replied in exasperation, sounding angry. "But I could no longer read her thoughts. I felt blindsided, Dad."

Bastion didn't respond. The uneasy feeling, he had in his gut all day long over the argument his son and daughter-in-law had the night before bothered him a great deal. He'd been disturbed by things she had said.

The sounds of movement in the adjoining room had both men whirling their heads toward the kitchen, rather than the front door where the figure still stood silently, unmoving. Appearing through the kitchen doors were Drayke and Kalabernus, two of Kahner's brothers. Both men glanced around the living room expectantly.

"Where is he?" Drayke exchanged uneasy looks with Kalabernus.

"Who are you referring to?" Bastion inquired, uneasy at the absence of his fourth son.

"Kalturek," Kalabernus supplied. "He said…"

"He said he had news." Drayke cut his brother off with an urgent headshake.

Moving toward Drayke rather than the door, Kahner grabbed him by the shoulder, forcing him to look him in the eye. Jaw clenching as his lips pursed angrily, he read his brother's thoughts, so prevalent on the surface of his mind. Shaking his head in denial as his breathing became ragged

Kahner backed away, tripping over his own feet as he fled toward the door.

"No! No, she wouldn't! She wouldn't do that to me!" Kahner hollered, his voice shaking. Reaching the front door, he flung it open. Seeing his identical twin brother's eyes shimmering back at him in a weary distressed state as well as a large black raven perched on the porch stair handrail, Kahner cringed. The presence of the bird was likely not a good sign. Stretching its massive feathered wings it cawed at him as if calling his name. This drew his attention to the flock of little black minions littering the yard. What were they doing here in the middle of winter? They normally vacated the valley during this time of year.

"They followed me in through the path as I arrived. Odd that, isn't it?" Kalturek didn't move. His eyes met his brother's as he stood, resting his shoulder against the doorjamb.

Kahner gazed at Kalturek with an imploring expression. "Kalturek, please tell me. Tell me she didn't do it," Kahner begged his brother, feeling slightly ill-at-ease. Kalturek may have been the youngest of the triplets but he was quite a formidable sight in his uniform.

With a pained expression and a heavy heart, Kalturek's gaze shifted past his brother toward his father. The look exchanged between the two men affirmed Bastion's worst fear.

"I'm sorry, Kahner. I found her at the clinic," Kalturek said, stepping into the entryway, holding papers in his hand.

A feeling of dread washed over Kahner as denial hit him full force. He slammed the door shut behind his brother, trapping the Raven King outside. "She wouldn't!"

"She'd already … already had the procedure," Kalturek stammered, his voice cracking as he spoke. He looked drawn, pale even, and his body began to shake. Batting at the snow from his Sheriff's uniform Kalturek could see his hand was beginning to tremble. He'd known this might happen. It was what he'd been afraid of; what he'd been trying to prepare himself for. But there was no preparing for a shared emotional response. Being identical twins, they were linked in more ways than one. During times of great sorrow or fear, they could feel what each other was experiencing emotionally.

In shock, Kahner stared at his brother. His skin drained of color. Chest heaving as panic and dread surged within, he ran his hands fervently through his hair in agitation. Crying out in anguish, he turned toward the living room. His hands balled into fists at his sides.

"No!"

Extending his hand with the papers toward his brother, Kalturek exhaled a shaky breath, hoping to pass on what he knew quickly before the full impact hit him.

"Eliza asked me to give you this."

"My wife just aborted my baby without my knowledge! What could I possibly want from her?" Kahner snarled. Pure unadulterated rage was building within him.

"Divorce papers," Kalturek responded evenly, gesturing with the documents toward him. "She said she won't ask for alimony. She'll figure it out on her own. As she put it, she doesn't want anything from you and doesn't figure you'd be inclined to give it anyway."

The silence that followed was deafening. Kahner just stared, his expression one of pain and bewilderment at the news.

"You know what? She's right," Kahner growled. Snatching at the papers, he yanked a pen from his brother's breast pocket of his deputy jacket. Rifling through the documents he scanned the papers hastily, placing his signature and initials where indicated. Then, thrusting the documents away and onto the floor, he stomped toward the kitchen, punching a hole in the dividing wall between the living room and foyer on his way. The impact of his fist crunching through plaster never fazed him.

"Kahner, wait!" Bastion called after him, afraid of what he might do. He fully understood the anger and betrayal his son was experiencing. They nearly mirrored his own.

It was an unusual set of circumstances. In Eliza's defense, his son had never told her of the family's abilities, let alone his own, before they'd married the year before. But to completely disregard his son's feelings and wishes about the impending baby had been unforgivable.

Scowling Bastion seethed inwardly with rage, wishing upon Eliza the worst of accidents to befall her. The child would have been the first of a new generation with gifted abilities, of which he hadn't even seen in his lifetime. But more importantly, it would have been the first of his grandchildren.

Turning back around near the kitchen doorway, Kahner growled angrily, "The witch took off! She took off and murdered my child behind my back!" Kahner spat, his words filled with venom, the wounded look in his eye evident in his tone as well. "I hope she burns in hell for this!"

As Kahner seethed with rage, Kalturek continued to shake violently. Moving quickly toward their brother, Drayke and Kalabernus took hold of Kalturek's arms on either side to help keep him from falling. His legs suddenly buckled underneath him. He would have fallen to the floor if his brothers hadn't been holding him up. The sheer weight of Kahner's pain and anger roiling within Kalturek's chest and head blinded him. Eventually, he blacked out.

Kahner's face drew tight and his hands clenched. He roared with rage, stalking from the living room into the kitchen, smashing lamps, picture frames and figurines in his wake. Pounding through the kitchen he ran out the patio door, cracking the glass as he shoved it out of his way, not bothering to shut the sliding glass door. Running at full speed down to the horse barn, he stumbled a few times in the snow. The icy cold seeped into his jeans, wetting them up to his knees. He felt nothing. Nothing but pain and agony at the loss of the one thing he'd wanted the most.

A child of his own.

A baby boy or girl.

Startling one of the handlers out exercising the horses before the next snowfall hit, Kahner forcefully grabbed the reigns of the stallion being exercised from his hands. Mounting the horse bareback he spurred it forward as tears stung his cheeks. The wind whipped across his face freezing them the instant they fell. He didn't care. Kicking the horse into a full gallop, Kahner gave an anguished cry as the sun began to set in the distant sky. Making a frantic run for the clearing that led to the trails, he was unconcerned by the near foot deep snow and his lack of a winter coat. The pain was too unbearable to endure any longer. Shaking uncontrollably, Kahner sobbed shamelessly, spurring the horse forward into a dead run. His father had always told him that real men don't cry. He knew in this instance, however, that Bastion would understand; his brothers too.

Back at the house, Bastion watched from the broken kitchen patio door as his son disappeared into the snow-laden tree branches near the trails. Sighing heavily, his gut clenched when he saw a very large black raven swoop down from the sky and land near his feet on the patio deck. Clearly it hadn't liked being shut out from view on the front porch.

"And what do you think you are doing here?" Bastion's tone was sarcastic. The birds head tilted up at him as he spoke to it softly, its black beady eyes blinking at him almost knowingly. It remained quiet. The eerie sensation that the birds presence and his son's recent loss was merely the beginning of a dark time in all their lives couldn't easily be dispelled.

Eliza's behavior of late had been erratic and uncharacteristic of her normal nature. The decision to abort her baby made no sense. She had always maintained that she personally believed such an act was unforgivable. What had happened to change her belief system so drastically?

Something was clearly amiss, but what?

Chapter 3

Indeed, what was amiss?

After what happened with Eliza, as you can imagine, Kahner had no desire whatsoever to have any kind of lasting relationship with another woman. This decision is significant to the course of events taking place at this point in the story.

Much to Bastion's displeasure, within days of the dissolution of Kahner's marriage to Eliza, his son announced that he wanted to apply for an entry-level position within the CIA. He'd spent four years as a detective for Loveland County, was apparently bored with the ease of his job, and was desperate to get away from his sibling's sympathetic platitudes and understanding stares. This was after discovering, by sheer accident mind you, that his father had at one time worked for them. Approaching his father with the request for a letter of recommendation Bastion promptly refused.

Kahner's anticipation that his father would put in a good word for him was quickly dashed and they argued for months. When Bastion realized, he wasn't going to be able to keep his son from applying, he finally agreed to help him, on one condition. He had to apply under an assumed name. Balking at the request, stating the notion he'd be able to get away with that was preposterous, Kahner continued arguing with his father. After several months of this he became fed up and anxiously accepted Bastion's terms, thinking if he were arrested for the fraud he'd at least be rid of the whole lot of his family. So, his father gave him a new identity.

Wait until you hear what name he gave him.

I'm telling you, you won't believe it.

Toni Starck.

Yes, you heard me right. He gave him the name of a comic book superhero - Ironman.

No. I'm not joking, and it is spelled with an 'I,' not a 'Y.'

Bastion RavenCroft obviously has a humorous streak in him. Of course, his children might argue it's a mean and sadistic streak when goaded.

They wouldn't entirely be wrong.

I'm betting at this point you're probably wondering why the need for the change in identity in the first place, right? I'd also imagine you're wondering how in the world Bastion was expecting to get away with giving his son a false identity – the name of Toni Starck at that – in order to enlist within the CIA without getting either of them caught? Am I right?

What you need to understand is that the entire RavenCroft family is gifted, not just Bastion and clearly, as hinted, Kahner, who is supposedly able to read minds. For that reason, Bastion was adamant that if his son were going to apply, and inevitably be accepted by the CIA, as he knew he would be, then Kahner would have to take up an assumed name just as Bastion had when he'd enlisted in the army many, many years before. That info right there is crucial to note. Bastion had enlisted with an alias and had gotten away with it. Impossible, right? You'd think but somehow he'd managed it and, therefore, knew how to effectively do it for his son as well.

It was imperative, you see, that the rest of the family was protected in the event Kahner's ability was ever discovered. For as Bastion, himself learned the hard way early on in his military career, such individuals, if found out by the wrong group of people, could be used for very dark purposes. Now, even though he was no longer in the armed service of the United States, nor working for the CIA, Bastion did still have, shall we call them, connections? At least for now, and that was how he'd get Kahner in under their radar. Who was his contact, you might wonder? Again, all in due course, yet still important, but I digress.

At this point in the story, we are now leaping forward almost fifteen years. It's the beginning of October. This is when many of the terrible troubles start. So terrible that it creates a big problem not only for Kahner and his family but for the woman he's been sent to protect as well.

I should tell you that Kahner has done well within the course of his clandestine services career. So well, in fact, that he is now working in undercover operations. His current assignment has him somewhere around Laredo, Texas near the Mexican border. To comprehend how terrible these circumstances become, one needs only to follow along. And remember, Kahner's name has changed to Toni Starck, so pay close attention.

- - -

Laredo, Texas
near Mexican Border
15 years later

Huddling near the warehouse building, they whispered back and forth, determining the best course of action. They'd been working undercover together now for the past three months and had managed to finally gain some ground. Kobi Radford's drug cartel may be vast, spanning five different countries but as recently discovered, he could be brought down.

It would take time, however.

Time Kalysta Radford and her children didn't have.

"You said she intended to come and get the logs from the computer?" Agent Toni Starck inquired of his partner.

Agent Ricardo Pegueros had been undercover within the cartel even longer than he had. Toni had simply been brought in three months ago to assist in getting Ricardo and the woman out. Unhappy in her marriage and deceived by her husband, Lionel Radford – having discovered his true line of business – Kalysta Radford wanted out.

"Oh, yeah. When I talked to Mrs. Radford last, she said she wanted to give us enough ammunition to put Kobi and Lionel away for good. She wanted to put an end to his 'tyranny and attempts at world domination.' Her words, not mine," Agent Pegueros responded. "Seemed pretty determined if you ask me."

"Ballsy, to say the least. And you believe her? Because she wants to get her kids away from Lionel?" Agent Starck's gaze shifted around the parking lot at all the trucks painted to look like postal delivery semis. They sat empty, awaiting their next shipment of drugs across state lines. It was smart really, the agent mused. Typically, not even cops would stop a postal delivery rig supposedly in route to the different post offices. Catching sight of a fox sitting near the wheels of a semi cab, he did a double take. The fox stared back at him, lifted a front paw as if pointing toward his partner then quickly disappeared. An uneasy feeling quivered in his gut then spread about his midriff. The warm sensation rippled up his back, curling over his shoulders and raced up the back of his neck. He cracked his neck in an attempt to dispel the sense of foreboding the presence of the fox had given him. He wasn't sure why, but the animal had spooked him.

Witnessing the odd exchange between Agent Starck and the fox, Agent Pegueros shook his head. "You know? You remind me of someone I've worked with before." He spoke unexpectedly, his accent giving away his Hispanic upbringing. Cupping his hands around his Glock he shoved the clip up inside.

Agent Starck was only mildly interested. "Really? His name Toni Starck too?" he mocked while adding a new clip to his gun as well. He shouldn't have been too surprised by the statement. It wasn't the first time one of his undercover partners had made such an assessment. It was one of the reasons he'd gone with the long hair and beard look as opposed to clean shaven with short hair. Not for the first time, he thought it odd but pretended to shrug it off.

"Nope. Franc Kastle."

Turning towards him, trying not to express too much surprise or interest, Toni tilted his head. "Did you say, Franc Kastle?"

"Sure did. Know him?"

"Can't say as I do." Toni feigned nonchalance. "Franc Kastle though. That his real name? I thought that was the name of that comic character, oh, what was it…?" Deep in thought, he scratched at his beard, still scanning their surroundings for any sign of movement. He needed a trim bad. It was itching something fierce and he was getting tired of having to maintain its shape.

"The Punisher you mean?"

"Yes, that's the guy."

"Interesting question coming from you, Mr. Toni Starck," Agent Pegueros smirked, finding his partner's question amusing. "How did you get that name anyway?"

"I'll say this much, my father seemed to think it was funny at the time. Even spelled the name in the effeminate with an `I' just to be difficult I'd wager." Toni's response was grim. Adding a clip to his spare gun he holstered it near his ankle. Hoping to drop the subject entirely and move on to something else, he situated himself where he could see the building better. Not for the first time was he wishing he could pulverize his father, for having given him the false identity fifteen years prior. It hadn't been until after he arrived at the agency when he finally learned why.

The reason had annoyed him.

He was aware the alias his father had taken up for service within the military and CIA had been Bradley Anthony Starck. What he had not known at the time was that apparently the man was still widely remembered as having a perverse sense of humor among many within the agency. The Director of the CIA, having crossed paths with Agent Starck on several occasions prior to receiving his nomination for directorship, in particular recalled his father repeatedly stating he hoped for a girl for his first child when he'd found out his wife was pregnant, so he could name her Anthony with an I. When Toni's application had come across their desk with his father's letter of recommendation and seal of approval, it hadn't come as too much of a surprise to anyone within the agency to learn he was the son of the famed prankster and sadist. Kahner RavenCroft had been going by Anthony Starck with an I, or Agent Ironman as many took pleasure in calling him, painfully putting up with the ribbing he'd been getting from the unfortunate name choice ever since.

He still marveled at how sympathetic everyone had been when within a year after he'd taken his job with the agency his father had been kind enough to fake his own death. Without warning him in advance – of course.

Agent Anthony Starck hung his head, bouncing it back and forth at the memory. His co-workers at the time had been most shocked and amused to learn that his father – who had been 82nd Airborne army ranger had managed to accidentally die while bungy jumping. The Director refused to believe it wasn't one of his warped jokes and ordered all kinds of tests done in order to verify it was really his dad who had died. He didn't even want to know how his father had managed to make *that* work because when the results had come back they'd been conclusive; Agent Bradley Anthony Starck had definitely died from a bungy jumping accident.

He received a formal apology from a very embarrassed Director shortly thereafter.

The following months after his dad's supposed death had been beyond torture and Anthony had no doubt Bastion RavenCroft, aka Agent Bradley Starck, had taken great pleasure knowing that would be the case. But his partner didn't know any of that; nor did anyone else but his father.

"Are you telling me he intentionally named you after a billionaire playboy comic character who wears tin cans and boosters on his feet?" Agent Pegueros asked in astonishment. He couldn't help but think all the man had to do was dye his hair black then trim his beard to a goatee and he'd be the epitome of the character he was named for. That is, if he weren't built like Thor and sporting the similarly long hair style and facial hair.

"What I think, is that he intentionally meant to make things difficult for me," Agent Starck responded with irritation, while internally cursing his father. More likely it was because Bastion RavenCroft had known they wouldn't believe him to be his son otherwise. Though, no doubt he'd still taken great pleasure at knowing he'd get a couple last digs in even after Kahner left Colorado. He'd known his father would have to fake his death at some point. They'd discussed it at length before he'd left, for too many questions would likely arise from Bastion's – or rather Brad Starck's – absence from the agency otherwise. The CIA still believed they lived in Kansas after all, and that his dad left the agency due to his mothers' death in order to finish raising his children in her absence, which was only partially true. They might try pulling Brad Starck back in, now that his kids were old enough to fend for themselves.

"What exactly did your dad do for the agency any-ways?"

Noticing movement out of the corner of his eye, he shushed Agent Pegueros with a finger to his own lips, pointing with his gun toward the lone figure near the front of the building.

"You know I couldn't tell you that, even if I did know." Truthfully, to that day Toni still had no clue what capacity his father had served within the agency. Employees of the CIA weren't exactly allowed to discuss that sort of thing outside the agency.

Swearing, Agent Pegueros tensed next to him.

"Is that her?" Agent Starck inquired, noting the near waist length braided caramel colored hair tucked down the back of her shirt, as well as her sultry gait. Dressed in black tight-fitting jeans and a snug t-shirt the woman's hourglass figure was extremely appealing.

"Yeah, looks different, though. Must have just dyed her hair. It had been dark brown." Placing the earpiece in his ear, Agent Pegueros continued. "Stupid woman. Why is she going through the front door? She has to know he'll get her on camera," he said irritably, pulling down his ski mask.

Gesturing toward Ricardo that he intended to make his way toward the building, they both went quietly, their mutual silence born of the need for stealth. Weaving back and forth through the postal trucks they reached shrubbery near the entrance. Waiting patiently, they watched her unlock the door and open it after entering the key code. Leaping over the wall as she slipped through the door, Agent Pegueros grabbed the handle with a gloved hand before it closed. Skirting through the door behind the woman Agent Starck reached around her, pulling her tight against his chest. Covering her mouth with his gloved hand to squelch her startled scream, he groaned when she kicked wildly at his shins.

"Calm down, Kalysta. He's my partner, Agent Starck," Agent Pegueros said quickly next to her ear, having pushed his way through the door. Pulling his mask up so she could see him, Agent Pegueros gestured for Agent Starck to do the same. He refused with a shake of his head, not caring whether it would put her at ease.

Heart thumping wildly in her throat, Kalysta Radford gasped for air on a sigh of relief when the agent released her mouth. Still holding her in a tight grip, she wriggled in his grasp angrily.

"Let me go!" she demanded in a harsh whisper.

Ignoring her demand Agent Starck slipped one hand down her side to her hip. Clasping his flattened hand against her belly to stop her squirming movements he spoke clearly into her right ear, tisking softly.

"Huh, uh. No way. Tell me where first," he ordered, not taking any chance this was a ruse.

Chin jutting out, her lip trembled and Agent Starck noted the bruising near her left eye and down the side of her cheek. She'd attempted to cover it with makeup, but it was still noticeable.

Giving the man a fierce look out of the corner of her eye Kalysta replied defiantly, "You guys gonna get me and my kids out of this mess, or what?" she asked heatedly, clearly refusing to go any further without their agreed assistance.

"Yes," Agent Pegueros assured her, tapping on his partner's arm in the process.

"Tonight?" Kalysta prompted further.

"That depends," Agent Starck replied, surprising his partner. "Are you going to go through with this, or are you going to back out last minute and leave us hanging?" he asked, trying to get a clear read on her. So far, he sensed little reticence at her willingness but sometimes battered women could trick him up. Holding her in place with one large hand, he reached up and pulled off the sunglasses that had gone askew during the struggle, then finally pulled up his mask. No longer necessary as nighttime had descended, he shoved the sunglasses in his pants pocket.

Staring up at the immense man holding her in place, Kalysta's breath caught in her throat. Inhaling sharply, she stared openly up at him, forgetting for the briefest of moments why they were all there in the first place. His soft brown eyes were by no means remarkable but his rugged good looks, on the other hand, had set her head spinning.

Feeling warm all over and unexpectedly at ease with him, regardless of her irritation at being grabbed from behind, Kalysta finally regained her senses and narrowed her gaze upon him.

"I think that depends on whether you're going to let me go. Or, are we just going to keep standing here potentially giving ourselves away?" Kalysta vented angrily. Her waspish response elicited a smirk from Agent Pegueros. Regardless of his good looks, she realized she had no business trusting Agent Starck. Her priority had to be the safety and well-being of her children.

Agent Starck could see the hate in her beautiful soft brown eyes and realized as he read her thoughts, that her desire to destroy her husband was great. Grimacing at her vengeful thoughts, he gave her one last calculating stare. Finally releasing her, he instantly wished his hand was still splayed across her belly. For a woman with three children, she had a mighty nice figure and she'd felt good in his arms.

Too good.

He was on the job.

Undercover at that.

And no woman could ever be trusted.

Trembling slightly at his touch, and from nerves for what she was about to do, Kalysta rubbed at her arms to ground herself. Agent Starck's dark masculine features under his beard had been an intriguing contrast to his long straight blonde hair falling into his eyes. It had felt good, safe even to be held next to him. Unsettled by the thought, she shifted her gaze away from him and peered around quickly. She attempted to determine the best way to gain access to her husband's office and, by extension, his brother's, and the accountants.

Following her down the corridor to the elevator Agent Pegueros halted her from pushing the button. "Is there another way up?" he asked, trying to ascertain whether their knowledge of points of entry and potential last-minute exits was accurate, as well as her legitimacy.

Gesturing further down the hall toward the exit sign hanging from the ceiling she replied. "That takes a person out back. The door adjacent is the stairwell. It leads up to all four floors."

Nodding understanding Agent Starck was pleased. They'd been over the blueprints and were already aware of logistics, but he could tell Agent Pegueros wanted to gauge her sincerity as well. Taking the elevator up to the fourth floor they first ventured into Lionel's office and gained access to his files. Then, heading across the hall to Kobi Radford's office, Kalysta saved the shipping schedules to a flash drive. Handing it off to Agent Pegueros, she then quickly and quietly led them out down to another office.

"What are we doing here?" Agent Starck asked suspiciously, noting a sign on the door listing Anthony Margoolis as the occupant.

Turning toward him, her darkening eyes flashed. "You want to nail Kobi and Lionel, don't you?" The contempt for her husband and his brother was obvious. "Andy's their accountant. I got his password this morning," she said smugly, stepping into an office which was just as vast as the last two. It seemed their drug money had bought them not only expensive computers and furnishings but expensive luxurious office space as well. Agent Starck noted the computer desk and hutch on the farthest side of the room and headed in that direction. He realized uneasily that it was an interior office, which meant there were no windows or exits other than the door they entered.

"How'd you manage that?" Agent Pegueros asked in surprise, oblivious to the grandeur of the room as he'd seen it all before. He knew full well how difficult Andy Margoolis could be and was aware of his womanizing ways. It was one of the reasons why there were no other exits to the room, which had always made him nervous. Andy liked trapping women in, so they couldn't get out.

Scoffing loudly, Kalysta replied. "All the men around here mistakenly assume I'm fair game since Lionel's taken up with a mistress. Even Kobi was pawing at me yesterday when I brought the kids by at Lionel's insistence." Seeing Agent Starck's cocked eyebrow and questioning look, she explained further. "Andy thinks I'm meeting him here tomorrow for a tryst. I fully intend to not be here," she said emphatically, recalling with distaste what she'd had to do earlier in the day, to get the password. The memory of the man's hands all over her chest and bottom caused bile to rise in her throat. Shivering the thought away, she concentrated on the task at hand.

Wading through Andy's vast array of porn, Kalysta managed to locate the appropriate files. Gesturing toward Agent Pegueros, he returned the drive to her, so she could save the files on one flash drive. Handing it off to Agent Pegueros once again, after she'd finished saving the documents, Kalysta stood and turned towards them anxiously.

"Now, get me out of here, please." She was nervous about how easy it seemed so far. "Before someone..."

"*Oy, Dios.*" Agent Pegueros said anxiously from the doorway. "We got a *problema, amigo.*"

Chapter 4

Kalysta froze, instantly on edge. Her breath caught in her throat once again as terror overwhelmed her. If they were caught, Kobi's men would kill them without question.

"What do you see?" Agent Starck's senses were on high alert.

"Two men, frogging back and forth at the far end of the hallway near the elevator. She must have been followed."

Eyes widening in alarm Kalysta became defensive. "That's impossible, I was very careful, and I even changed my hair!" she exclaimed quietly, grabbing hold of her braid still tucked in her shirt. She stood within a foot of Agent Starck. Gun in hand; he'd positioned himself instantly in front of her.

From the other side of the office, Agent Pegueros peered over at the two at the desk. "I can make it to the exit before they see."

Waving his arm toward him, Agent Starck urged him on. "Then go," he encouraged, watching him disappear as he spoke.

"Wait! Why is he leaving without us?"

Becoming hysterical, Kalysta attempted to rush towards the door. Halting her, Agent Starck grabbed her by the waist and tackled her to the floor behind the desk. Leaning towards her, he moved to kiss her only to be shoved unceremoniously away.

"What are you doing?" Kalysta whispered, giving him an odd look.

"I need a distraction," he explained, leaning up over her once again. "You're good at that, right? It's how you got the password," he whispered next to her ear, sending an unwanted thrill up her spine.

Kalysta stared up at the handsome man in distress as he proceeded to yank off his shirt. Her eyes became saucers at the sight of his immense muscular chest. Gulping, her first thought was, he was built like a bear. And the thought of kissing this stranger held more appeal than she cared to admit.

Thinking quickly Kalysta analyzed her situation. She was positive she hadn't been followed, so she figured they'd tripped an alarm somehow.

- - -

This is where I must break in ever so briefly. At this point in the story, Kalysta is feeling desperate. So desperate in fact, that she makes an extremely inappropriate suggestion as to how they might get out of this situation. Suffice it to say, Agent Starck takes her up on it, and though it goes no further than some heavy petting, with them both being scantily clad, it did, unfortunately, mean being viewed by the men while in a compromising state.

Now before you judge, you should ask yourself, what would you do to survive and get back to your children? Would you compromise your beliefs to save your own life and that of someone sent to protect you and your kids? I'm by no means saying its right. That said, one could argue that present-day situations force individuals to have to make choices they might not otherwise make in the heat of a moment. Choices of which we usually tend to regret later.

- - -

Realizing they now had an audience Agent Starck clasped his Glock within his hand, grateful for the feel of the cool metal against his fingertips.

"Get out of here!" Agent Starck roared. He turned towards them, cross at being interrupted regardless of the ploy.

Standing in the office doorway were two of Kobi Radford's men. Their hands rigidly gripped 50 caliber guns. Relaxing their posture, at the unexpected sight of the woman, they became distracted by the view before them.

"What are you doing here?" One of the men demanded, waving toward them in disbelief with his gun, silencer already in place. The man's neck craned to see more of the woman.

"Isn't it obvious?" Agent Starck asked, mocking incredulity as he stood erect. He deftly lifted Kalysta up from the desk, being sure to hide his gun behind her back. His expression was neutral, but he sensed she understood the silent apology he was trying to pass on.

Distracted by the view before them Radford's men were not prepared to react to Agent Starck's actions. Reaching behind him with one hand he flung the envelope opener he grabbed, hitting the man nearest the doorway square in the chest even as the man raised his gun. The henchman fell backwards to the hallway floor. In the same fluid motion, Agent Starck raised the gun in his hand and shot the man next to him, placing two silent rounds in him, one in the head then chest. The shot the henchman made swung wide, the bullet whizzing past Agent Starck's head by barely a foot even as the man crumpled to the floor.

Moving around the desk to a better position Agent Starck took his gun up in both hands. The shot made little noise, for Agent Starck's gun had a silencer, but the muffled hollow whizzing sound still hung in the air. Putting a bullet in the head of the man lying in the doorway with the envelope opener in his chest for good measure, Agent Starck peered back toward the desk.

Catching sight of Kalysta as she attempted to huddle behind the desk, Agent Starck never skipped a beat. Taking swift steps back towards her, he then took hold of Kalysta's arm. Instructing her to keep her eyes closed, he hastily dragged her up from the floor where she'd been cowering behind the desk attempting to redress. She was shaking visibly but moved quickly in step with him as he directed her towards the door. Moving past the body near the doorway he directed her gaze towards the hallway, so she couldn't see the carnage on the office floor.

Agent Starck paused, glancing from one length of the hallway to the next. Guiding her towards the emergency exit, they escaped to the other side. They paused momentarily, leaning against the wall next to the door as he peered back through the glass window in the door. Hearing shouting coming from the other end of the hallway on the opposite side of the emergency door, Agent Starck grabbed her hand and pulled her towards him down the stairs, still holding his gun at the ready.

"We gotta go. Now!" He declared in a loud whisper.

"I have no socks! Or shoes for that matter!" She cried out in a hushed tone.

Agent Starck grinned. "All the better to see those pretty polished red toes," he said, eliciting a scowl from her face. Almost laughing aloud over the look she gave him, he continued down the steps, groaning in disappointment at the sight of her now jean-clad legs.

"You had to leave your shoes rather than your shirt," he called back jokingly. He missed seeing her scowling back at him as he urged her on with a gesture of his hand as they went.

Perspiration beaded along Agent Starck's brow as she followed quickly after him down the stairwell in silence. The muscles rippled across his back as he ran, stole her attention. In his haste to get her out, he'd left behind his shirt. She realized her heart had been pounding in her chest from the moment Agent Pegueros had announced they weren't alone. Fear of being caught and being able to get back to her children had spurned her decisions in the moment. She couldn't believe what she had tried to convince Agent Starck to do to her.

Though still married to Lionel it was hard for her to experience guilt over the inappropriate suggestion she'd made. Her husband had been a cruel liar who'd been sadistic in beating her. Kalysta had attempted to escape him once four years before, only to be caught and brought back to him. He'd beaten her in front of her three children as a lesson. She'd sworn from then on, she wouldn't go against him again just to save her children from ever having to witness his violence. But when Lionel had hit her ten-year-old daughter Lisa, over a spilled bowl of cereal last Friday, she'd decided all bets were off. Beating on her was one thing. It was still wrong of course, but at least as an adult, she had a better chance of defending herself. Her children on the other hand...

Anger surged within her at the memory of her daughter's screams as Kalysta reached the bottom of the emergency stairwell. Trying to shake it off and bring herself back to what was happening in the moment, she took a deep breath. She was embarrassed by her behavior with Agent Starck, but where her children were concerned she would do anything. Kalysta knew she had to get them away from Lionel. It had become obvious to her that they were no longer safe with him.

He'd always sworn he'd never touch them.

That he'd never hurt them.

But then it wouldn't be the first promise Lionel had ever broken.

"Kalysta, where are you?" Agent Starck asked. He waved a hand in front of her face upon reaching the bottom of the stairs. Where moments before had been a strong woman, capable of quick thinking and action, was now a trembling fragile china doll, easily broken with a slight tap.

"What?" Kalysta's eyes refocused on him. Shaking her head, she cleared her throat. "Right, sorry."

"Don't lose it on me yet." Agent Starck said earnestly, trying to keep his own self in check. His encounter with Kalysta had affected him more than he cared to admit. Shoving through the door he grabbed hold of Kalysta's arm, took a quick survey of the alleyway then encouraged her out the door.

"You've been doing great, Kalysta. Now, where are your children?"

Chapter 5

Retrieving the three sleeping kids from the mini-van, Kalysta had parked several blocks away, Agent Starck assisted in transferring them to another vehicle.

After making sure the children were settled, he took hold of Kalysta's elbow, guided her into the front passenger seat and buckled her in, pulling the seatbelt tight. So far, the children hadn't awakened. He suspected she might have given them something to help them sleep.

Walking around the front of the vehicle after shutting her door, he was about to slide into the driver's seat when a shifting shadow drew his attention. Homing in on what had caused him to pause, he noticed a small animal sitting at the base of a dumpster. The creature sat up on its haunches, its head raising proudly to attention. It occurred to him it was likely the same fox he'd noticed in the parking lot. Feeling instantly alarmed and pressed for time he growled, swearing loudly and removed his earpiece. Tossing it to the pavement, he smashed it to smithereens with the heel of his shoe.

"What are you doing?" Kalysta asked in alarm.

Getting hastily into the drivers' seat, he shut the door louder than intended, started the engine and shifted the vehicle into gear.

Once could have been shrugged off as a coincidence, yet an odd one at that considering the area and region of Texas they were in. But twice in the same night in the span of thirty minutes? Any time a fox had ever appeared in his life it meant a potential danger loomed ahead. He wasn't about to take a chance and ignore it.

Sensing, rather than feeling Kalysta's movement next to him, he gave a soft sigh of resignation. Keeping his gaze forward, attuned to the road and their surroundings, he spoke.

"Don't do it."

Kalysta gaped at him, her hand clenching around the item she'd lifted from the console between them. "You knew I took your gun?"

"Yup." Agent Starck tried to keep from grinning. "I figured you having it might make you feel more secure for the moment."

Met with silence, he shifted his gaze cautiously towards her. Seeing her peering back at him suspiciously through her long lashes he gave her a querying look.

"Could you take this from me? Forcefully that is?" she asked.

"In a heartbeat," he said without a second thought. He looked back at the road.

Eliciting a disgusted snort, she dropped the gun unceremoniously back into the console between them. "Right, because now I feel really secure," Kalysta vented. "And you never answered my question."

Inhaling deeply Agent Starck quickly determined how much he wanted to tell her for now. Such cases were always a challenge. People going into witness protection never fully understood what was happening in the moment, especially with all the television and movie misinterpretation of how things played out.

"We will not be meeting up with Agent Pegueros again," he explained. "His assignment ended with the retrieval of the files you were so kind to aid us in getting."

"But I thought he was going to help me disappear." Her tone was resentful.

"He was present to facilitate our introduction and retrieve the files. Nothing more," he said firmly, sensing Agent Pegueros had not explained things too well. Aggravated by the notion, he continued to inform her of what was happening. "You and your children are now in my protective custody. My job is to take you to a safe house and keep you in hiding until I determine a safe place for you to relocate."

Inhaling a trembling breath at his words, Kalysta sagged into her seat, resting her head against the window near her ear. A strangled laugh escaped her throat. "I'm not sure there is such thing as a safe place away from Lionel and Kobi," she said morosely. "When Lionel discovers I'm gone, and Kobi learns what I've taken, I'm a dead woman."

Lifting her head, she glanced over at Agent Starck, distress clear in her eyes. "Ah, who am I kidding?" Her head swiveled from side to side as she spoke frankly. "I was dead from the moment I made the decision to dye my hair."

Casting a furtive glance her way he tried to reassure her. "I *can* keep you safe. You and your children are in no danger while in my presence."

Shaking her head, she stared out the windshield, her eyes glazing over with unshed tears, her voice becoming hoarse as she spoke. "No. No, you really can't. But whatever happens to me, Agent Starck, you have to promise - no matter what - that my children are never harmed by Lionel ever again."

Disturbed by her statement, he grimaced, recognizing instantly why she had made the decision she had.

Something had happened to one of her kids.

Staring straight ahead he continued to probe gently into her mind, attempting to ferret out what had prompted her desperate departure from Lionel's life. Clearly, he had been abusing her. That was obvious by the bruises on her face. But until recently, he assessed, he hadn't touched the children.

The daughter.

Yes, that was it.

Lionel had struck her daughter.

And when Kalysta discovered his business ventures were of an illegal nature, she made the decision to flee with her children, knowing full well he might find her anyway. But why? Why did she believe she would be discovered, he wondered?

As if she were reading his thoughts Kalysta spoke up suddenly. "You can't take me to just any safe house," she said quietly, sounding as though she were about to crawl into a hole and never reappear. "Kobi has people."

"Meaning?" Agent Starck asked, already sensing what he'd suspected for some time now.

"*Meaning,* there's a mole in your house. And they aren't in the basement or mail room," she said in answer, staring him down. The seriousness of her words was enhanced by the ghostly pallor that had instantly taken over her complexion.

"I see. You know who?" Taking his eyes off the road briefly as he asked the question, he caught the look on her face as she bit her lip. She was trying to hide it, but unsuccessfully. Kalysta knew but was afraid to tell him. Unfortunately, for her, she thought her mind was a private place.

It wasn't.

He could delve within and see, or hear rather, what she was thinking.

Ripley Braddock.

Hitting the brake pedal harder than he intended at the next light, Agent Starck shot a startled look her way, unable to completely mask the surprise upon learning who it was.

"Kalysta, are you sure of who you think it is?" Agent Starck asked carefully, trying hard not to give away that he knew. "Do you have proof?"

Fidgeting in her seat Kalysta's gaze moved to the windshield, unable to look the agent in the eye. But the tears welling in her eyes hadn't been lost on him. Taking a deep breath, she replied in a small voice, "Yes, I have proof," she said, then paused, "and it's damning."

Whistling softly under his breath, Agent Starck realized instantly the true danger she was in. The individual in question, Ripley Braddock, held a high-ranking position within the CIA and he was one of only a handful who had access to WITSEC relocation information. He suspected he now knew the second reason for the fox's presence. The scheduled safehouse was already compromised.

He was pretty sure he already knew what the first reason was for the fox seeking him out. The timing of the animal appearing coincided with the conversation he'd been having with Agent Pegueros before meeting Kalysta. What he'd said had disturbed him a great deal. His mention of another man within the bureau, with a name from a comic book character, who had reminded Pegueros of him, had him on edge. He'd been thinking strongly as they moved through the building, gaining the material needed to take down Kobi and Lionel Radford, that it was high time to disappear. Neither warning could be ignored.

He knew what he had to do.

Making a calculated decision, he pulled off ten minutes later into a small privately-owned used auto dealership. Parking the vehicle next to a Jeep Cherokee, he instructed Kalysta to keep her head down and quickly transferred everyone again to the jeep. Wiping down the vehicle, steering wheel and all, he then wrenched open the driver's side door of the SUV and ripped the door panel off, grabbing a small vinyl packet from inside. Tucking the packet down in his duffel bag, he threw on a spare shirt from within, re-wiped down the door and panel for good measure, and tossed the bag into the jeep near Kalysta's feet.

Hot wiring the vehicle, he hastily drove away. Continuing for another fifteen minutes, he managed to locate a similar vehicle and stole its plate, placing it on the jeep. Returning to the driver's seat they took off once again.

"Agent Starck, what's happening right now? Is this normal procedure for a relocation?" Kalysta asked, confused by the lengths he was taking. She'd imagined half a dozen agents would come with dark sport utility vehicles and would ferret them away in the night to some secluded cabin in the woods.

Not answering right away, Agent Starck stared ahead, formulating what it was he wanted to say. The conversation with Agent Pegueros before meeting Kalysta had disturbed him a great deal. His mention of another man within the bureau, with a name from a comic book character, who had reminded Pegueros of him, had Agent Starck on edge. He'd been thinking strongly as they'd moved through the building, gaining the material needed to take down Kobi and Lionel Radford, that it was high time to disappear.

Long ago his father had warned him when he'd first given him his identity to enlist in the service, that he might need to disappear someday without warning. It was why he had given him the new identity. Agent Starck couldn't help but wonder as he drove Kalysta Radford to safety if his father had foreseen these events happening. Like his grandmother

Sapphire, Bastion RavenCroft had the gift of "Knowing" after all. That's what she'd called it anyway, knowing things without knowing how or why. To some extent, he had received a bit of the gift himself along with the ability to know people's thoughts.

"No, Kalysta. It is not," he finally replied.

"I take it you're taking me seriously?" she inquired, seeing him nod. "Why? You don't know me from Adam, or for that matter, Eve. I mean, not that I'm objecting but why would you trust anything I say without proof?"

Halting at a red light before entering the freeway, Agent Starck peered over at her evenly, his expression blank. "You're mistaken, Mrs. Radford, if you think I ever believe anything any woman ever says," he said coldly.

Feeling blasted by his statement and the ice in his tone, Kalysta shivered in the cold vehicle, suspecting its lack of heat was due to a faulty heater. Schooling her own features so they remained as passive as she could, she responded in kind.

"Well then, you'll understand why I, a woman and Lionel Radford's former wife, never take anything a man ever says at face value."

Hearing the dark chuckle at her words she went on. "It would seem, for the moment, that I am at your mercy."

Deferring his head toward her, Agent Starck replied mildly, "So it would seem."

Anxious at the lack of emotion in his voice Kalysta stared at him momentarily, his profile she reflected, just as handsome as the view of him from straight on. Becoming uneasy at his continued silence and lack of forthcoming information, Kalysta's stomach churned painfully.

"Just keep in mind," she said, clearing the knot from her throat, "There are three innocent children involved here," she stated, holding a hand to her queasy belly, hoping upon hope that she hadn't made a poor decision.

"Of course, how could I possibly forget?"

"And don't ever call me Mrs. Radford again," Kalysta finished, narrowing her gaze upon him angrily.

"As you wish. But just so we're clear. As far as everyone else is concerned, Kalysta Radford is dead. You are now Laney Stevens. At least for now."

"What do you mean for now?"

"Oh, there will be multiple names and identity changes, so get ready to keep it straight. But for now, it's a pleasure to meet you … Laney Stevens."

Chapter 6

"What are you doing?" Kalysta exclaimed fifteen minutes later. Recently dubbed Laney Stevens by Agent Starck, she was having difficulty adjusting to her new name.

Met with silence, the man next to her barreled the vehicle along, having turned off the road. The jeep was creating its own path through the grassy open plain between El Indio and the Camino Columbia Toll Roll. Turning his head briefly towards her, Agent Starck could tell the woman next to him did not like his plan.

"Wait! You're not taking us into Mexico, are you?" Moments before her daughter Lisa began to stir as she slept. Kalysta was hoping she'd stay asleep a little longer but suspected with all the moving around they'd been doing she might wake soon.

"Have a problem with Mexico?" Agent Starck inquired, gunning the vehicle forward. He knew this section of the border was hard to patrol and a much more likely location to cross. Smugglers had been moving guns through for quite some time in that area. The key was finding a spot they hadn't already traversed regularly, to avoid the smugglers themselves.

Turning green in the face Kalysta's stomach churned painfully. The last time Lionel had taken her and the kids into Mexico she'd become violently ill. Claiming the water he'd given her had been safe, he'd taken pleasure in watching her get sick, much to her children's alarm. That had been six months after her attempt to escape. She'd learned fast after that not to accept anything he gave her that had already been opened.

"No, no, no! Not Mexico! You can't take me and the kids there. We'll get sick!"

"Won't be here for long. Few days at best," he shrugged.

Eyes widening in alarm she cried out in distress, no longer caring if she woke the children. "No! I am not spending five minutes there. Let alone a few days!"

"Oh, okay." Careening the jeep to a sudden stop Agent Starck moved to turn off the engine.

"What are you doing?"

"Stopping so you can get out."

"Wait. What?" she asked in alarm. "You can't just dump us here," she exclaimed angrily. "What do you think you're doing?"

"I'm going to Mexico to disappear. What are you doing?"

"Agent Starck, are you telling me you're relocating me and my children to Mexico? Cause Agent Pegueros never said anything about…."

"Agent Pegueros is not here and you have never heard of him. Got it?" Agent Starck declared harshly. "As for me, I am no longer Agent Starck. Get it clear in your head. From now on I am your husband."

"Over my dead body."

"That can be arranged."

Toni's response was quick and clipped, completely void of emotion; his voice holding within it a tinge of menace.

Shoving back against her seat toward the window Kalysta stared back at the dark presence before her. "Are you kidding me with this?"

"I assure you, I rarely joke about anything," Agent Starck said wryly. "Now, make a decision. You have ten seconds. You want to be stranded at the border alone with three kids, or in Mexico with me?"

"Two such appealing options. Gee, which do I choose?"

"Five, four, three…"

"Oh, just go already," Kalysta exclaimed angrily. Tears filled her eyes in her anger, and she struggled to push down the fear she was experiencing. Feeling a hand patting at her leg she jerked in her seat, grasping the door handle and hand rest tightly.

"I will get you somewhere safe," he said quietly, noting the terrified look in her eye and wary mannerism. "But you must trust me."

"Trust is earned, not freely given," she responded shortly. Kalysta gazed at him out of the corner of her eye, as she held her roiling belly.

Harrumphing softly Agent Starck, who was looking forward to eventually re-emerging once again as Kahner RavenCroft, shook his head and turned away. Her words haunted him, for they were the same his father had spoken to him, the last time he'd seen him.

- - -

Six hours later they pulled up in front of what appeared to be a small abandoned single dwelling adobe home with a clay tiled roof. Parking the vehicle close to the front of the hut Kahner exited the vehicle and checked out the house. It was dirty and appeared to have been used as a way station for immigrants crossing the border. Hastily removing the carcass of a small dog from a dilapidated table, he tossed it out back behind the adobe home for the time being. He'd bury it later once he had the children settled.

"We're staying here?" Kalysta had asked at first.

The look he threw her way, as he grabbed his bag from the vehicle, halted any more questions from her lips.

"Right, no questions just do what you're told," she mumbled under her breath. In other words, no different than when she was living with Lionel.

Kalysta had no idea where they were and was too uneasy to ask. By the time they'd arrived at the adobe home the tension inside the vehicle had become palpable. At one point, not long before they had stopped, Agent Starck had picked up his phone for what seemed like the hundredth time and began texting again. Shortly after, she'd heard Agent Starck chuckle humorlessly next to her and speak for the first time in a while.

"It would take more than that," he mumbled under his breath while shoving his phone toward the center console with a scowl. Sliding over to the opposite side it had dropped down next to her feet. Reaching for the cell phone automatically, Kalysta had attempted to grab it up for him only to be propelled forward when he stomped on the brake pedal. Smacking her head hard against the dash, she cried out and cradled her head instead, glaring at him angrily.

"What did you do that for?"

"Never touch my phone," Agent Starck had said fiercely. His eyes narrowed upon her. Then more softly, "Sorry about your head," he said. Reaching across the console, and her, he'd deftly picked the phone up with his long well-muscled arm. It had been the closest contact they'd had since their encounter on the desk in Anthony Margoolis's office. Their eyes met briefly, and she suddenly somehow just knew that the contacts he was wearing were colored.

Now, where had that come from?

- - -

Where Indeed?

But the fact that Kalysta, or rather, Laney, as he was calling her now, came to the odd revelation about his eyes isn't what's so terrible. No, that would be the situation, Toni Starck, aka Kahner RavenCroft suddenly found himself in. You see, what had originally been a simple relocation assignment just became a three-ring circus. There are several things happening here.

One, his partner, Agent Pegueros, has just inadvertently tipped him off that there is another man in the agency who looks and acts a lot like him. In the back of his mind, he's realizing that this is the third agent within the past six months who has made this observation. And now he has a name to put with the illusive man; Franc Kastle.

Why is this significant?

Because first, unlike his siblings, he knows that his father's brother had, at one time, worked at the CIA too, but was thought by Bastion to have retired. For reasons that will be explained later, Kahner's uncle, Rafe Blackthorne, is not aware of him and his siblings because he is also unaware of Bastion's existence. Were Rafe to find out there could be serious trouble for the whole family. And second, and most troublesome, is the fact that the individual in question is using a name of a character from a comic book series called The Punisher. Any of this starting to sound vaguely familiar to you?

Franc Kastle?

Toni Starck?

Now, what would be the odds that his Uncle Rafe might have the same warped sense of humor as his father? High odds considering Rafe and Bastion are born of a set of triplets just as he and his brother's Kalturek and Kalabernus were. Taking into consideration the knowledge that Rafe is the same age as his father and, therefore, too old to be working undercover work anymore, it is highly probable he's got a cousin working within the agency now.

Right about now, I'm sure you're probably asking why this is so important? Well, let's think here. The RavenCroft abilities are hereditary and Kahner is aware that his uncle Rafe has six children as well, all similarly gifted. The question was, which one could it be? And did he want to stick around long enough to find out? Because if it was the mind reader, like him, then the quiet lives and relative secrecy that his family had been enjoying would likely come to a grinding halt.

Nope.

No way.

It was time to disappear.

He was prepared for this, his father had made sure of it, but first, he had to deal with Kalysta and her kids. The problem with that was, the woman had just informed him of yet another issue within the agency; a mole. Ripley Braddock, the head honcho of WITSEC, apparently was in Lionel and Kobi Radford's pocket. Mind you, these are drug Lord's we're talking about here, and as a result, some dangerous men. If Kahner were to take her to the designated safe house, she would be dead within the hour and her kids would be back with their extremely violent father.

Granted, he and Agent Pegueros had seen to it that it appeared Kalysta and her children were killed in a plane crash just before taking off with them. They'd even gone to the extreme of bringing in bodies so there would be bodies in the wreckage and subsequent rigged explosion.

Gruesome? Yes, definitely, and no I'm not going into detail as to how they did it. Just know they did.

Under normal circumstances that would have been enough for it would have looked like one of their drug competitors had taken out his estranged family. Now, on the other hand, it was clearly not. He imagined Lionel Radford had likely received the news of their deaths at the same time he'd driven her into Mexico. Ripley Braddock, however, would know that was a ruse. Just killing her on paper was no longer enough. So now Kahner had to figure out a way to make her disappear off the face of the earth, or Lionel Radford could find her and the children.

Just terrible, right? Absolutely terrible. Horrible even, or awful.

Huh, maybe I should have come up with a better title. Ah, well. Terrible Karisma works too, either way. Trust me. Because charisma is one ability Kahner had been sorely lacking.

Third, and not the least of Kahner's worries, is his dilemma on how to go about making them all disappear, himself included. Did I mention he needs to do this without her getting wise to his own sketchy identity, his abilities, and without inciting his father's wrath?

Add all this to his highly annoying attraction to Kalysta, of which he's trying desperately to temper, and you can see we have a recipe for disaster. Wouldn't you say?

But don't you worry.

He'll figure it out.

Sort of.

Because the chaos isn't over yet.

Chapter 7

The next day.

"Your dead."

The moment he said it Kalysta instantly flinched. Palming his Glock from his left to his right hand, he tilted the barrel toward the floor.

"Time to go, tooth lady."

Extricating himself from the bench he'd been sitting at near the table while he cleaned his gun, Agent Stark grabbed his bag and slung it nonchalantly over his broad shoulder. Tucking his gun down the back of his jeans he headed for the door.

Kalysta peered down at the elk tooth necklace she always wore around her neck. It had fallen out from under the t-shirt he gave her the day before. Hearing the door open, her head snapped up when she realized he was leaving.

"Kids, up, up! Get up, quickly. We have to go." She attempted to rouse their sleepy heads as she raced toward the door. Her heart was in her throat. He hadn't even bothered explaining his cryptic answer to her question. Now he was heading out of the Adobe hut he brought them to before sunrise that morning, like he intended on leaving them behind. She didn't know a lot about the Witness Protection Program, but she had to believe that leaving the witness and their children behind was in somewhat bad form. What in the world was going on?

"Wait! Agent Starck," she called loudly.

The man spun around just outside the door, his face registering anger. "Don't ever call me that again." His foot propped the door open so he could see inside. He noticed the kids had dirt smudges on their faces and clothes from having slept on the floor.

"What the heck am I supposed to call you then? You *are* Agent Anthony Starck, aren't you?"

Cocking his head as if he had to think about it, he backed out of the hut. "That could be debated. For now, call me..." He stopped. Absentmindedly patting around his hip, he reached back, yanked out his wallet from his back pocket and pulled a card from within. He read off the name. "Devilin A. Dress."

Kalysta couldn't help it. She smirked. "Okay, I'll call you devil in a dress, if you insist."

Lisa gave a yawning grin as Jordan giggled, his face alighting with mischief.

"Hey, Adam, it's like the song Dad would always play when Uncle Kobi came over to drink. You know the one? Devil in a Blue Dress?"

"It's Devil *with* a Blue Dress." Lisa corrected before Adam could.

"Is that really your name? Devilin Abludress?" Adam asked. They woke briefly when they first arrived but had surprisingly fallen asleep again shortly after introductions.

Toni Starck's head fell back, his body went lax, and he groaned outwardly as he spoke to the heavens in disgust. "Really? First it was Anthony Starck with an I, and now this?" Jamming the ID in his wallet as he fumed, he returned it to the rear pocket of his jeans. He was pretty sure his Dad had great fun putting together his packet of fake ID's. An issue he fully intended to address with him when he finally got home. First, he had to relocate Kalysta and her children.

Sensing movement to his right, Starck promptly shut the door and grabbed for his gun. Aiming toward the nearby bushes he focused in on what had drawn his attention. At first he thought he was seeing a small dog staring back at him until he noted the grey coat with rusty tones, a black tip to its bushy tail, and the distinctive markings around its nose.

Another Fox?

In Mexico?

It was different from the one he'd seen in Laredo, Texas. They stared at each other momentarily. The fox lifted its head toward him, then shifted its gaze back down the road heading East as if it wanted him to go that way.

They'd just come from that direction that morning. He frowned, taking in his surroundings, he peered both directions down the road that ran east to west. Getting a nagging feeling in his gut he hollered back at Kalysta who was standing in the doorway peering at him in confusion.

"Devilin, is it? What are we doing here? The kids are just waking up and no one has eaten a thing..."

"Get everyone out of the hut and into the vehicle."

She didn't like being ordered around. Becoming cross she swiped at a strand of her hair that escaped her braid and glared at him. "You never explained..."

"Not now, Kalysta. I've the sense we need to be getting out of here."

Her eyes widened. Calling back at her kids, they all promptly scrambled out of the hut and made their way noisily into the jeep Cherokee, grumbling about being hungry.

Starck winced. They really needed to switch out that vehicle pretty soon. Particularly since they were driving a stolen vehicle with a stolen plate in Mexico.

Tossing his duffel bag in the back end, he quickly slid into the jeep. Spinning the vehicle back around he took off.

"Wait. Didn't we come from that direction this morning?"

"Yes."

"Then why aren't we going the other direction?"

"The fox said to go this way."

She stared at him. "Is that like ... code or something?"

"Nope."

"So, we're talking to a fox now?"

"Yup."

"And taking directions from him?"

He turned his head toward her briefly, his long, dirty blonde hair fell around his face. "Don't be so sexist. It might have been a her."

Her expression was blank. The kids in the back seat didn't know quite what to make of the conversation, or, for that matter, the man.

"That's just great." She fumed. "Devilin A Dress is talking to a female fox and taking directions from it. Lionel is liable to catch us for sure at this rate."

Starck reached over and patted her on the leg, the contact seeming oddly affectionate to him for some reason. He pulled his hand away. "Amanda, Honey, I told you. You're dead."

"Yeah, you said that a little bit ago. Wait ... Did you just call me Amanda?" It had taken her a second to register what he called her.

"Yes, Amanda, my love?" His response was sugary sweet. "My lovely wife, Amanda Dress, who is happily along for the ride on a much-needed family vacation."

She made a face at him.

"What? I could have called you Iwanda."

Her lip quirked up on one side at the terrible name and pun. "Explain the whole being dead thing again."

"I never actually explained it the first time."

She gave him a warning look.

"If you must know ... before Agent Pegueros and I met up with you at Lionel's office we headed over to the hangar where he houses his Embraer Phantom Jet and set it up for a guy to take it out, supposedly hauling a cargo of four, and head toward Roswell, New Mexico where it's going to crash down in a field about three miles north of there."

"Why near Roswell?"

"What better place than near a space he, and emergency crews, won't be able to get to right away?"

At first Kalysta didn't understand what he was talking about. After repeating the Roswell name several times, it occurred to her, the location he was referring to had to be near the sight of the supposed alien aircraft crash of 1947.

He nodded, when he saw understanding in her expression. "Yup, the famous Area 51. Your flight plan lists you heading to the nearby Mescalaro Reservation where your Grandmother's sister still lives. Elkhart, Texas seemed a bit too obvious a location for you to choose to hide. But the location the pilot's bailing out at will give us a little more time to get you gone before anything could possibly start appearing suspicious."

"Makes sense. Though when they don't find any bodies it's going to be obvious we're still alive."

"Who said they won't find bodies?" The ominous knowing look he threw her way had her shivering even in the heat of the day. They had their windows down, hoping for some relief since the air conditioner in the vehicle wasn't working.

"So when you said 'a cargo of four' you really meant..." Her voice trailed off, leaving what was better left unsaid, unspoken.

"Does that mean ... Daddy's gonna think we're dead?" Lisa asked from the back seat.

"Yeah, Honey, sounds like it," Kalysta said softly.

"Good." Lisa huffed. Leaning back against her seat, her arms hugging her chest protectively, she scowled darkly at the door handle. Her two brother's looked at each other than back at their mother, who'd turned away and was now resting her head against the seat belt.

Starck suspected, whatever incident had prompted the mother to escape with the children, had affected the girl adversely. She clearly had no qualms about leaving her father behind. Sensing the boys, however, had mixed feelings on the matter, he tried to engage them in a game of Once Upon A Time as they drove. Pretty soon he had all three kids giggling and laughing as they played along even with their mother.

The jeep Cherokee jiggled and shook over the rough terrain of the dirt road causing them to jostle about. Fortunately no one was prone to carsickness. It didn't, however, keep their minds off of how hungry they were getting.

"Agent..."

"Stop."

"Sorry. Devilin A Dress."

The kids giggled loudly.

Starck grimaced. "Devilin is sufficient for today." He couldn't wait until he was able to switch out his name with one of the other ID's.

"We need to stop somewhere to get something to eat."

The last thing Kalysta wanted to be doing was eating or drinking anything in Mexico after her last experience. But she knew it was inevitable at some point.

Chapter 8

Two and a half very looong days and multiple name changes later.

- - -

"Reservation, sir?"

"No, just need a room. List it under Randulf Blackthorne," Kahner RavenCroft said, thinking it odd his father had given him this particular ID. He'd been trying to avoid using it, but it was the last one he had in his packet.

The new name was meant to fit the new look he was sporting. His hair had been dyed brown just the day before. It was now slicked back and tied in a very short ponytail at the nape of his neck. His colored contacts had been switched out for pale green ones, and he was now wearing dark glasses. Looking like, a cross between a writer or movie producer, he shifted his weight against the check-in counter, lazily awaiting the key to his hotel room. Trying to look simply bored rather than desperately in need of respite and a good night's sleep, he yawned into his hand.

"Yes, sir," the front desk clerk replied. "I have a room with double beds available. Do you have any pets and is there a preference for smoking or non-smoking?" the man asked casually. He peered up at him briefly. Short and thin, dressed in khaki pants and a white pull-over shirt, he appeared too young to be staffing the front desk of the Budget Host hotel.

"No pets and non-smoking preferred. We're going to need a roll-away bed and I'm guessing extra towels," Kahner responded. Kalysta had been complaining for the past two days about wanting and needing a real shower or bath for her and the kids. So, he'd finally given in and pulled into the hotel. He needed a few hours of sleep himself and figured a shower afterwards might help wake him up for the remaining drive.

Kahner had stopped briefly last night while still in Mexico to deal with changing their hair color and to give him time to create new identities for the kids and Kalysta. Arguing over whether Kalysta needed to cut her hair, she'd finally acquiesced after he'd dyed her hair black. Insisting that she could cut it alone, she'd kicked him out of the tiny gas station bathroom where she'd been attempting to get a sponge bath. Returning from the bathroom ten minutes later, he'd been satisfied to see her hair was in a surprisingly thick shoulder-length braid.

Finding a secluded location to park the vehicle for a while so he could sleep for a bit he'd woke early at around four in the morning and decided it was best to move on while the rest of them slept. After crossing the border into New Mexico just west of El Paso, Kahner traded the 2013 Jeep Cherokee for a badly rusting yellow 1989 Chevy Lumina. Waking Kalysta and the kids with the news that they needed to switch vehicles, she had been severely annoyed with him to discover the vehicle they'd traded for had no heat. As it was January, even southern New Mexico tended to be rather cool in the early morning hours. Recognizing the need to keep everyone warm, he'd purchased a couple used blankets from a nearby second-hand shop.

"Of course, Mr. Blackthorne," the clerk said, regaining his attention, bringing his thoughts back to the task at hand. "I'll have everything down to your room shortly."

Running a hand across his face as he accepted the key card to his room, Kahner noted the number on the key listed room three.

"Thank you. You have me in…?"

"Room three, Sir."

"Is that near the office?"

"No, Sir." The young man smiled, pointing out the picture window across the way. "Numbers start on the opposite side. You can park in front of your room."

Acknowledging what he said with a slight nod, Kahner turned on his heels and walked back out the hotel door to his awaiting vehicle. Noticing Kalysta fidgeting in the front seat, he suspected she wasn't going to like his new plan much more than she had liked the one about taking the route through Mexico. But then she had limited choices considering her situation. She was, after all, the one stupid enough to get involved with Lionel Radford of all people.

Reaching the vehicle, he gestured for her to get out. "If you can carry your daughter, then I can get your boys," he said, opening the side door. All three children had fallen asleep in the back seat, having become bored with the long drive. What normally would have been a six and a half to seven, hour drive had turned into nine hours as the result of the need for frequent rest stops for the kids.

Rubbing at her sleepy eyes Kalysta pulled Lisa out from the opposite side, eliciting a tired moan from her daughter.

"Are we there yet, Mama? I'm so tired of driving."

"So am I, Honey. I'm not sure how much longer but look here. We get to stay in an actual hotel room tonight with a television," she said, trying to put a positive spin on the situation. Seeing Kahner shake his head at her, as he carried the quickly waking twins to the door, she faltered. "Wait a minute, aren't we? I thought that was why we were here," she said as she set her daughter down.

"Consider it a way station. Like every other stop we've had," Kahner let them into their room. Bending down he set the boys on their feet since they had awakened as well. Hurrying into the room the three kids dove for the remote control, desperate for a chance to watch cartoons. Closing the door on them so they could speak privately Kalysta held the key loosely in her hand.

"Agent Sta…"

"Stop," Kahner halted her with a hand in the air. "It's Randulf Blackthorne while we're here."

Sighing in exasperation Kalysta stamped her feet. "So many names, I can't keep track! And the kids and I need a break. We've been driving practically non-stop for three and a half days now."

"Look, I get it, Angela."

"Did you call me Angela?"

"Yes, it's your name here."

"Soon you'll be calling me, what? Mother Mary?"

"I can give you the name Mary in the next state if you like."

"Randulf is it now?" Kalysta asked sharply, becoming irritated and tired of the constant daily name changes, and new rules he was forever giving her. Seeing him defer his head in assent she continued. "I appreciate what you're doing here. I truly do. I would never have gotten this far if it weren't for your assistance. But me and my kids, we're not like you. We cannot keep up this pace."

Crossing his arms over his chest he stood looking down at her almost wearily. "I get that you all are tired of being on the road, but the pace we're going at is necessary and…"

"Randulf!" Kalysta exclaimed, losing her patience. "Give us a break. We need a break!" Her brown eyes flashed behind the green contacts he'd given her. Turning away she moved to push the room key back in the door to unlock it.

Staring at Kalysta's neck closely Kahner's eyes narrowed to slits. He hadn't paid much attention that morning when she'd awakened and sat up next to him. But now he noticed a section of hair coming loose from her braid. Becoming suspicious he reached out and took hold of her hair. Yanking out the hair tie, he started pulling at her hair.

"Stop! What are you doing?" Kalysta hollered in a panic while pushing through the door.

Kahner's face became pinched and the muscles near his neck flexed as he clenched his jaw angrily. "Blast it all, Woman! I told you to cut your hair," he said, raising his voice as he shut the door behind him loudly.

Squealing as she shoved his hands away from the hair falling from her braid, Kalysta took several steps back. The silver pendant – surrounded by two elk teeth – that she had tucked underneath her shirt came loose from its hiding place and flashed at him brightly.

"Give it to me," he demanded, his eyes widening angrily at the sight of the thin leather corded necklace she'd managed to hide so well. He had told her to get rid of that thing. Extending his hand toward her, he stared at the front of her shirt.

Glancing down nervously, Kalysta cringed when she realized he was staring at her necklace rather than her chest. Clasping her hand around the pendant protectively, as Adam and Jordan gazed between their mother and Kahner anxiously, she awaited his impending wrath.

Not wanting to make a scene in front of the kids, Kahner took her forcefully by the arm and hauled her to the bathroom. Closing the door behind him, he forced her to sit down on the toilet seat.

"Are you trying to kill yourself? And your kids?"

"No, of course not!"

"Could have fooled me. Leaving your hair like that shows a blatant disregard for the safety of your own children. And this…" he vented, yanking the pendant and chain from her neck.

Yelping at the feel of the thin leather cord snapping against her skin, her hand flew up to the sore spot left behind. "You broke it," she cried in distress as she bent forward. Seeing the braid pull loose from its hairpins and flop down her back Kahner took a firm hold of it, bending it near the nape of her neck. Mad that she'd disobeyed him and put them all at risk he grabbed his pocketknife from his front pocket, slid it under the braid between his fingers, and sliced through it.

"What are you doing?" Kalysta gasped as she cried. "No. No!" Becoming hysterical she kicked at his leg to try and get him away. "Stop! Please don't," she begged.

"Knock it off," Kahner growled, holding the braid in his hand in front of her face.

Seeing her hair separated from her head Kalysta's face contorted in agony. Grabbing frantically at the back of her head her eyes darted about the room in a daze, as they succumbed to the welling tears. She wept bitterly, sobbing as she slid to the floor in front of the toilet in a heap.

"Woman, it's just hair. It's not like I cut off your right arm," Kahner said in dismay. Looking from the braid in his hand, then back to the woman in despair on the bathroom floor, his gut clenched uneasily. Feeling more than a bit guilty at cutting it off the way he had, he turned slowly, figuring he'd better give her a few minutes.

Closing the door behind him he stepped past the vanity into the room. Seeing Kalysta's children huddled on the bed together he watched as they became visibly upset at the sight of the braid in his hand.

"You cut it. You actually cut Mama's hair?" Lisa exclaimed in horror. Her small hand flew to her mouth and her eyes filled with tears.

"Lisa, calm down. Your mama is fine. I only cut her hair like what she was supposed to do yesterday. I didn't hurt her." Kahner tried to explain calmly.

"You're wrong," Adam piped up angrily, balling his little fists in his hands. "You're so wrong if you think you didn't hurt her just now," he hollered.

"Look, kids, this is how it works," Kahner defended himself while trying to get the kids to understand. "Your mama's hair was too long and would tip off the bad men trying to get her. Remember what we talked about?"

"You mean Daddy," Lisa said giving him a knowing look and angry scowl. "No point in trying to pretend otherwise. We know what kind of man he is. We've known since the day he nearly killed Mama."

Sitting quietly behind the other two children, Jordan stood and walked around the bed. Pulling himself up to his full height, he stared at Kahner disdainfully, as he stuck his hands in his pockets.

"If you just killed our mother, then I'll never forgive you," the little boy said. He struggled to fight back tears of his own as his lip quivered worriedly.

Becoming exasperated Kahner dumped the braid in the nearest trash can, making a mental note to be sure and burn it later. "I didn't kill your mother. As you can plainly hear by her caterwauling, she's very much alive."

The little boy stood before him shaking his head. "You got no understanding of what you just did, do you?" Jordan said in disgust as he peered bravely up at Kahner.

Sensing something was amiss Kahner frowned. "Jordan, son, what are you talking about?"

"Mama's told us the same story ever since we were little. She said a messenger came to her in a dream once, a long time ago before she ever met Daddy."

"Yeah, she wasn't even out of high school yet," Adam added.

"And the messenger told her never to cut her hair. Then later before she went off to college her grandma warned her not long before she died never to cut her hair too."

Scoffing Kahner gave them a disbelieving look. "You're saying an angel told her not to cut her hair?"

All three children nodded their heads in assent. "He said the longer it was the stronger she would be," Jordan explained fervently. "And that if she ever cut it... Well..." stopping abruptly, he eyed his siblings uneasily.

"If she ever cut it, what?" Kahner prompted, his curiosity getting the better of him as he sat on the bed near them. He was getting that uneasy feeling in the pit of his stomach again. He didn't like it at all and he was feeling more than a little guilty for cutting it as her apprehension and anxiety over it being cut had likely stemmed more from her Native American grandmother's warning then any angel she might have dreamed of. Learning that bit of her background along their drive through Mexico had not only explained her dark coloring and bone structure but the unusual pendant of elks teeth and a cross he'd just yanked from her neck. It was indicative of her unusual heritage and, well, her, which was why it needed to go.

Taking a deep breath Lisa finished the story, her face screwing up painfully in distress. "The messenger said if she ever cut it, her life shortly after would end, for she'd lose all strength to fight."

Feeling as though he'd been punched in the gut, Kahner cringed. He wasn't exactly the believing sort, and yet, at the same time, had always respected the beliefs of those who did. He recognized that just because he personally did not believe in such things, it did not necessarily mean they might not be true.

Frowning, while running a hand across his face in agitation, he got up from the bed. "Look, guys, you have to keep in mind that this is just a story. Just because she said it happened doesn't mean it did. You guys are safe with me. All of you, including your mother. Nothing and no one will harm you while I am around. Understand? That's why we have to go to such lengths."

"But her hair was her strength," Lisa said urgently as tears poured from her eyes in distress, clearly very upset at the loss of her mother's hair.

"No. A person's strength is right here," Kahner explained, thumping gently on her chest with two fingers. "And here," he continued, tapping at the girl's head gently. Taking her face in his large hands he peered gently down at her. "One's heart and one's mind is their greatest strength. And the only thing that can take that away is if a person stops believing in their own ability to survive. Okay?"

Nodding their heads slowly and solemnly, the children stared at Kahner as if appearing lost.

"Your mama's going to be fine. She's upset it had to be cut. But she will get past it."

"For your sake, I hope you're right," Jordan said quietly, his voice barely above a whisper.

"Jordan, what are you talking about?"

"Mama also said the one who cuts her hair, will be the one to end her life."

Stunned, Kahner simply stared.

Chapter 9

Kalysta was extremely disoriented when she finally woke up the next morning. Initially, she didn't remember where she was. They'd moved around so much in the past several days and had stayed in some shoddy places. But somehow Agent Starck, Randulf Blackthorne, or whatever his name was now, had managed to locate and afford, at the very least, a clean motel.

Sitting up slowly in bed she peered around her room while carefully removing her daughter's arm from across her hip. A faint pink and golden light streaked through the sliver left between the window hangings. She squinted in the early morning light of the sunrise. Noting the boys were breathing soundlessly next to her in the other twin bed, her gaze shifted to the empty cot shoved against the wall between the window and the boys' bed, where they'd removed the table to fit it. Hearing noises coming from the bathroom Kalysta became annoyed. How was it that man could not only wake before her but move so soundlessly that she didn't hear him get up? Living with Lionel she'd had to learn to wake at the tiniest sound, never knowing which man she'd run into; the gentle quiet one or the hateful violent one.

Rubbing at her eyes Kalysta yawned then realized she'd left her pants on the other side of the bed. Throwing the blankets off her in a panic, she crawled out of the bed nearly tripping over her own feet. Her legs felt weak and unsteady for some reason once she'd finally become untangled. She lost her balance. Falling to the floor she cried out in surprise at the pain she experienced in her right leg. She was a bit dazed and trying to push up to a sitting position when she saw Agent Starck fling open the bathroom door just to find her sprawled on the floor.

"Are you all right? What happened?" Surprised to see she was only wearing a t-shirt and underwear, Kahner's eyes roamed over her bare legs in appreciation. He knelt on the floor next to her.

One of Kalysta's boys moaned then rolled over in their bed, grabbing both their attention briefly. Soon they'd be waking, wanting to watch cartoons on the television before they left.

"I fell," she said stupidly. Tucking her legs up under her, she made unsuccessful attempts to cover herself with the baggy t-shirt. She looked up at him and was startled by what she saw. Her eyes widened in appreciation. He was freshly shaven with his hair dyed black and cropped short-GQ style. His appearance had been drastically altered by the close shave and haircut he'd given himself.

And for the better indeed.

If she'd thought he was sexy as hell before, it was nothing compared to the heart-stopping view she had of him now. Bare-chested, clad in nothing but jeans, Kalysta was once again given the pleasure of viewing his well-muscled arms, shoulders, and chest. Her appraising gaze roamed along his collarbone up toward his well-chiseled, wide features. His lips drew her attention. The sudden desire to lean forward and kiss him caused her instead to draw back and glance further up his face.

Staring up at the immense man before her, Kalysta's breath was cut short by the sight assaulting her senses.

Inhaling sharply her eyes widened in surprise.

Oh.

My.

Word!

She stared openly up at him, forgetting for the briefest of moments that she hated this man with every fiber of her being for having cut her hair.

Agent Starck's eyes were nothing short of mouth dropping. The softest of blue, like the palest of crystal-clear diamonds, they weren't harsh but bright as the light she imagined one would see at the end of their life. Feeling warm all over and unexpectedly at ease with him, regardless of her irritation at finding herself half-naked before him again,

Kalysta finally regained her senses and narrowed her gaze upon him.

"Agent Starck, those are your real eyes, aren't they?" she stated in amazement.

Somehow, she sounded almost hopeful.

Chuckling, the man before her reached over and patted her hip. "Yes, they are," he responded, all the while appreciating the sight of her bare legs. "And the name is Kahner now. Stop calling me Agent Starck," he said evenly.

"But yesterday afternoon you said your name was Randulf."

"Randulf Blackthorne. Yes. But that was yesterday. This is today. With the new look comes a new name."

"Suppose that means since you whacked my hair off I've got a new one too?" she asked bitterly. Reaching up self-consciously, Kalysta had to fight back tears when she felt the tips of her hair so close to her chin.

Leaning back on his haunches, the man who had finally returned to his true self, looked at the woman before him. For some reason, today she seemed so much more fragile and he didn't like it. She appeared more drawn than usual and her demeanor was almost submissive, despite the bite in her tone.

"Look, Kalysta…"

"Oh, so we're back to Kalysta are we?"

Swearing Kahner scowled. The woman could make him slip up faster than a rabbit on thin ice. "Sable, don't do that. Your hair didn't define who you are. You haven't lost your strength. You're the same woman you were yesterday."

"No, I'm not."

Taking hold of her arm to halt her before she could move away, Kahner forced her to look at him. "Yes, you are," he said firmly. His eyes bore into hers.

Shifting her gaze away from his mesmerizing pale-blue eyes, she peered around quickly, determining the best way to extricate herself from her awkward position on the floor.

"You said it yourself, Kahner," she responded, saying his new name forcefully. "Yesterday, I was, Angela. Today I'm, what was it again? Oh, right. Sable?" Jerking her arm out of his grasp, as if he'd burned her, she came up off the floor in a huff, not caring anymore that she was only wearing underwear and a long t-shirt. Grabbing up her pants from the floor she hurried on past him.

"Now, if you'll excuse me. I need to use the restroom."

Disappearing into the bathroom, Kalysta shut the door behind her. Leaning up against the counter for support, her arms shook as she stared at the woman in the mirror. She no longer recognized. Herself. The quick jagged cut from the day before had left her hair in quite a disarray and the black coloring, as far as she was concerned, was unappealing. She'd always had a deep tanned skin tone, often kissed with a reddish hue when she'd been out in the sun too long, but now next to the stark black hair coloring she couldn't help but feel it looked unnatural under the harsh light in the bathroom. Especially since it made her brown eyes appear even darker.

Taking a ragged breath, she stripped and stepped into the shower. She needed to feel the hot water against her skin. Maybe then she wouldn't feel so dead inside anymore.

Reaching automatically for the pendant that usually lay against her chest for comfort, she began to weep in despair. Sobbing uncontrollably, she allowed the water to roll across her back. Resting one hand against the shower wall, and the other against the empty space at her chest, Kalysta choked on a sob. Consumed by her grief, the loss of her hair, and her grandmother's pendant, she was unaware of the presence within the bathroom. Kahner pulled back the shower curtain and entered the tub.

- - -

Whoa! Wait a minute!

He entered the tub?

That's right, unfortunately, you didn't hear the story wrong.

We make well-meaning decisions when we see someone in pain, which often turn out to be questionable at best. That's what happens here. Unable to handle hearing her crying, Kahner attempts to console her. Can we say, wrong place, wrong time?

What starts as a gesture of consolation turns into something highly inappropriate under the circumstances; an intimate exchange. Now, one cannot and should not judge them, for as the author of this story is so kind to point out, anyone can make a poor choice in the heat of the moment; no matter what your background, faith, or upbringing.

Except me, of course.

I never make bad choices.

You know, because I'm perfect.

I am Vortigern Black after all.

Hahum. Anyway…

One could argue that Kahner wasn't attempting to console Kalysta, rather he was trying to find some peace of his own, for truth be told, she wasn't the only one in pain. Kahner had been struggling with his own anger, resentment, and fears ever since the betrayal of his ex-wife, Eliza. Nearly fifteen years he'd been bottling up all that emotional trauma, and he had never allowed himself to fully cope with the loss of his wife or the child he would never know. So, when two people in pain meet, find themselves in an intense situation, confined within proximity, and you add a highly charged attraction between them, one could potentially find them-self in a heap of trouble. Wouldn't you agree?

I would imagine, you all can probably figure out what all wound up transpiring here. I offered to give the skinny on the hot and heavy. Even tried to argue the point that some might not have a good imagination where such things are concerned, but the author seemed to think this was sufficient.

Did I tell you how exasperating she can be yet?

See now, I told you things were going to get more complicated. Let's just be honest here, it was likely inevitable that it happened as they had been fighting the attraction for the past three days.

What do you think Kalysta, or rather, Sable's reaction is going to be if she finds out who he is? Or rather, that who he is now *is* who he is. Or wait...(scratches head)...awe heck, you get what I mean.

After making such a choice as they have, though, how do you suppose they manage to keep her children from catching them? Let's find out, shall we?

- - -

Relinquishing his hold of her Kahner set Kalysta back down so her feet found the smooth wet surface of the bathtub. He leaned into her as her back stayed pressed up against the shower wall. Their eyes met, each appearing slightly startled by what had just happened between them as the water continued pouring down upon them.

"Oh, my..."

"-Word!"

"What have..."

"-we done!"

Finishing each other's sentence, they stared back at each other in dismay.

"You...you were just so upset," Kahner said defensively.

Kalysta stared wide-eyed back at him in horror. "I didn't mean to..."

"I was only trying to console…" he said while kicking himself internally.

"Mama? Are you in there?" They both froze at the sound of Lisa at the bathroom door. Panicking, Kalysta whirled around to turn off the shower just as Kahner halted her hand on the knob. Her feet slipping beneath her, she found herself being hauled back up into his arms briefly as he righted her in place.

"Answer her," Kahner whispered roughly against her ear.

Stammering, Kalysta replied. "Yes, Baby. I'm in here!"

"Can I come in? I gotta go potty."

Covering her mouth with her hand in horror Kalysta gaped up at Kahner, unsure what to do.

"It's okay, Lisa. Come on in," Kahner called out to her. His expression was impassive but Kalysta detected a slight amount of mischief in his pale blue eyes.

There was a slight pause and then a response. "You're in there too, Randulf?"

"Yes, Lisa. But it's Kahner now. I'm just helping your mom with her hair in the shower. If you need to go, then it's okay, come on in," Kahner replied. He hated lying to the girl, but the truth seemed highly inappropriate for her young ears.

"It's, Kahner, now you say? Right. Well, okay then," Lisa said softly. A cool shaft of air wafted into the bathroom as the door opened. They could hear her hurry in and lift the toilet seat. The sound of small bare feet dancing in place could be heard briefly then it was quiet but for the sounds of a young girl humming softly.

What seemed like forever actually only took a brief minute. Noisily dropping the lid in place Lisa flushed then attempted to scamper from the bathroom.

"Lisa, did you wash your hands?" Kalysta called before the girl escaped, eliciting an exasperated look from Kahner.

"Really?" he whispered harshly, his eyes narrowing on her.

Wide-eyed, Kalysta shrugged back at him as if to say, 'What do you expect? I'm a mother after all.'

"Oops, right." Running back into the sink, Lisa turned on the faucet and quickly washed her hands while Kalysta and Kahner stood in the shower waiting impatiently for her to exit.

"What are you two doing in there anyway?" Lisa called to them as she turned off the water and began drying her hands.

"I'm just helping to trim your mama's hair, so it's shaped better," Kahner replied, rolling his eyes to the ceiling. "Figured it was the least I could do after yesterday."

"In the shower?" Lisa inquired, sounding confused.

"You know hair always cuts better when wet," Kalysta responded, becoming exasperated herself. "And there's less mess in here then. It'll just wash down the drain."

"Oh, right. Okay." Placing the towel back on its rack Lisa turned and headed for the bathroom door. "Guess I just figured you both were making out," Lisa said, disappearing through the bathroom door, closing it behind her.

Groaning, Kahner hung his head as Kalysta's shocked gaze attempted to peer through the solid off-white curtain. A hysterical giggle bubbled to the surface.

"It's not funny," Kahner scowled down at her.

Struggling to keep from smiling Kalysta stifled a laugh. Gazing back up at him she was struck once again by his amazing eyes.

"It's … it is a little funny," she giggled, unable to stop herself. At the same time, she couldn't help but be disturbed that her daughter even knew of such things already.

"You just be glad I left the scissors in my shaving kit rather than on the counter. Otherwise, you'd be explaining to her how I was cutting your hair without scissors."

Laughing, Kalysta ducked out of harm's way. He attempted to lunge for her playfully even as she tucked the towel tightly around her, suddenly feeling self-conscious.

Kahner threw the curtain back realizing he'd have to switch jeans at some point or it was going to be a very uncomfortable drive.

"Best get to that haircut then I guess. We need to get moving." Reaching for his shaving kit, he pulled out his scissors only for them to be snatched from his hands.

"Oh, no you don't. You don't get to go anywhere near this hair again with any kind of sharp implement." Giving him a dark look, as if to say he'd be marked for death if he attempted to come near her, Kalysta stood her ground.

Raising his hands as a white flag, he moved around her in a fluid motion toward the bathroom door.

"No worries. The bathroom is all yours now," Kahner said. Snatching a towel off the rack on the door, he draped the towel around his shoulders. "Try not to take too long." His expression became impassive, where before it had been animated. He opened the door and backed away as though attempting to distance himself from her.

"If you'll be all right then, Sable. I know two other people who will likely be waking soon." Kahner put his hands in his pockets and stepped out the bathroom door. Turning, he stayed there as if waiting for her to follow.

"Right," Kalysta said, feeling a bit stung by his formality. "Wait, what did you call me?"

"Sable. It's your new name from here on out."

"My new name is definitely, Sable, then?" she asked in surprise. "Is that permanent?"

"Yes, from here on out, Sable Kryder is your name. Until Friday anyway."

"Wait, what happens Friday?"

"I'll let you know," Kahner responded evasively, not wanting to go into detail just yet.

"That is kind of pretty – the name that is," Sable said on an exasperated sigh, tired of being in the dark about everything. "Where did you get that?"

"Do you really want to know?" His brow rose questioningly.

Flushing, she replied, "No. Guess not."

Leaving her to trim up her hair and dress, Kahner shut the door behind him, while trying to shake the image of her naked body from his mind.

Chapter 10

Sable peered into the mirror and cringed. She noticed there were bags under her eyes and her hair was a mess. Finding a comb in Kahner's shaving kit, she ran it through her short hair, to attempt some semblance of order. It had been a long time since she'd had to trim her own hair, but she managed to even it out all around. Adding an angled cut to the hair around her face, she then dried it with the complimentary hair dryer, noting that it at least framed her face nicely now.

Throwing her clothing back on, she was grateful that she was fully dressed when she saw Kahner was waiting impatiently on the bed with a cup of coffee in hand. She shifted uncomfortably; suddenly shy due to the intimate exchange they'd shared.

"What time is it?" she asked, noticing the faint sunlight trying to peek through the shades he'd drawn the day before.

Her children were munching on doughnuts while drinking cartons of chocolate milk.

"It's just after seven thirty. You took a little longer than I anticipated."

"It takes a little bit to trim one's own hair when not used to having to do so," she sniped back. "Have they been awake long?"

"They've only been awake about twenty minutes. But they have been asking about you, Sable."

The use of her new name was intentional, to remind them both what it was. He watched her closely. His gaze narrowed upon her, as though he were trying to ascertain what she was thinking. Shaking the silly thought from her head she moved carefully around the bed, attempting to skirt around him without touching him.

Reaching out, Kahner took hold of her arm in a firm grip, effectively halting her progression. "Sable, wait," he said quietly. His voice was smooth this morning, and his demeanor was casual.

"What?" she asked cautiously. From her experience when men were trying to be nice to her, it meant they wanted something from her. Since he'd already gotten from her what most men were usually after, she couldn't imagine what else he might desire from her.

"I am sorry about the hair."

"No biggie." Sable tried shrugging it off, even as her face registered distress.

"According to your children, it is a huge deal. They think I intend to kill you for some reason."

Noting her tan complexion drain of all color, Kahner scowled. "What is it about this story they're telling me? Some angel…"

"Just forget it. It's nothing."

"It sure seems like something."

Limping as she moved past him toward the bedroom doorway, Sable grimaced. The ankle had turned on her awkwardly when she'd fallen before the shower. It was going to become an issue she realized, which was a problem. If she ever had to run for it, she wouldn't be able to. Choosing to ignore his statement she attempted to open the door of the motel room.

"Did you really see an angel when you were eighteen?" Kahner asked finally, his curiosity getting the better of him.

Hand cupping the doorknob, Sable paused and looked back at him finally. "Yes."

"Where do you think you're going?"

"Coffee. Unless, of course, you were thoughtful enough to grab me one?" she stated, quirking her eyebrow at him doubtfully. Noticing him grimace and glance toward his own cup, she shook her head in disgust. Disappearing through the door without a backward glance, she shaded her eyes from the glare of the sun and started walking. The woman now calling herself Sable Kryder desperately needed coffee, and she knew she could get it from the vending machine down the hall.

Returning to the motel room a few minutes later, Sable opened the door and called out to her children in greeting.

"Good morning!"

"Morning Mama," all three of her children chimed back at once, not bothering to lift their heads from the glued state in front of the television screen. Sable noted, they were all dressed, and their shoes were already on as if they were ready to leave. They all got up from the bed as Lisa turned off the television.

Setting her coffee cup on the table near the door, she embraced them all in a gigantic hug when they came forward to greet her, then proceeded to kiss and hug each one in turn.

"We're about to leave again, Mommy," Adam said.

"Yeah, we were worried you wouldn't get back in time," Lisa said, glancing over at Kahner who was already grabbing up the bags and checking the room for anything left behind.

"Mommy! Mommy!" Jordan exclaimed, waving at her as he pointed at his hand. "Look! Donuts for breakfast."

"Daddy Kahner gave them to us." Adam nodded happily.

"*Daddy* Kahner did, did he?" Sable emphasized 'daddy' humorlessly. "Yes, I noticed he'd given them to you before I left. You all were too engrossed in your cartoons to even see me leave, I'd wager." She looked back in his direction as Kahner exited the bathroom after one last check. Her eyebrows rose at the sight of him, though her expression changed suddenly, and she seemed to fidget where she stood.

The man should not be that good looking.

Honestly, it should be illegal.

"Yeah, they are so yummy. You should try some," Jordan replied. He lifted the doughnut box up in her face, distracting her only slightly from the view.

Kahner stood before her, loaded down with all the bags while trying to balance his coffee cup. He peered over at her and grimaced again while clearing his throat. He seemed to be doing that a lot lately.

"Still learning what all they like and well, you know, I figured kids and doughnuts go together right?"

"Obviously," Sable said in a snappish manner. Realizing she was being unfairly harsh she softened her tone. "Donuts are fine. As you can see, they love them. I warn you, they tend to make them hyper though."

Kahner's eyes grew and he glanced towards the kids, watching them as they chased each other around the motel room.

"I'll have to remember that. Sorry."

Sable shrugged, "No problem, you didn't know; though I'm betting you made friends for life," she chuckled, glancing their way as she heard Adam shriek over being tackled by Jordan. "Besides, I should have been out here for them when they woke. Can I help you with anything?" she asked almost shyly as she watched Kahner move towards her, weighted down with all the bags. Sable could feel the hairs on the back of her neck stand on end as well as goose bumps on her arms when he passed close by her.

"No. I've got it. There's breakfast if you're interested," Kahner said, shaking his head at the donut box in her son's hand. She nodded her belly rumbling at the notion. Figuring her need for caffeine and food outweighed any discomfort she was feeling being near him, she gestured for her kids to follow as they meandered out of the motel room door.

Chapter 11

"Sugar?" Kahner offered. He handed a cup of take-out coffee to Sable who was seated next to him. They had stopped at a drive-thru thirty minutes later in deference to their need for further caffeine. Shaking her head, she accepted the cup gratefully and took a sip.

"I much prefer maple syrup," Sable stated.

"Are you serious?" Kahner looked over at her and laughed aloud.

"Yeah, I know I get that a lot," she sighed. "Waitresses are annoyed by me."

"They're probably just as annoyed with me as they are with you then." He reached through the window and accepted his own coffee cup from the attendant. "You sure you don't want anything for the kids?" he asked.

"Not unless you want them forcing us to stop every thirty minutes like yesterday. Trust me; one shared water bottle is fine."

"Fair point."

Pulling away from the drive-thru window, Kahner parked briefly to get situated. Reaching into his duffel bag next to him, he pulled out a small bottle of maple syrup, eliciting a quirked eyebrow from Sable.

"My private stash," he explained. He tilted the bottle into his own cup then took Sable's cup from her and added some to hers as well. Stirring it in, Kahner handed it back.

Taking a sip, she smiled appreciatively. "That's perfect, thank you," she said as he nodded in acknowledgement. "I've never known anyone else to like maple syrup in their coffee before."

"Just means the rest of the world has poor taste," Kahner grinned, taking a drink from his own cup. "Not the best but it'll do. I noticed you were limping to the car earlier." He glanced over the seat at the children who were reading their respective books. They seemed content for the moment. Pulling back out onto the road, he kept going. They'd be heading into the country soon and there was a pond he'd seen on the map not far away. He needed to get to it soon before the hour got too late. The less traffic when he dumped the car the better.

She shrugged it off. "It's nothing, just bruised maybe."

"I can look at it if you like."

"No," she said sharper than she'd meant to. Seeing his almost wounded expression she took a deep breath, "I just don't want to be a bother any more than I already have been," she responded, eyeing the doughnut box on the floor near her feet.

"It's no bother and you should eat something," Kahner encouraged, noting the direction of her gaze. Seeing the distressed look on her face, he let it go for the time being. "Maybe later, if it's still bothering you."

"Okay," Sable responded weakly and reached down for the box. "Maybe just a long-john."

Kahner smirked. "Thought you already had one of those," he said playfully.

"Oh, you're evil." Sable dropped the box back on the floor in disgust.

"What? Aren't you going to have one?" Kahner chuckled.

"I'm not hungry anymore."

She was clearly irritated by the innuendo.

Just then Kahner's cell phone beeped. Grabbing up his phone he noted they would be coming up on the pond in a few minutes.

"Do me a favor and be looking for a small pond off to the side of the road. It might be enshrouded by trees."

Nodding, Sable gave him a curious look but sat intently gazing out the window as she drank her hot coffee. He had pulled up a map when they first headed out of the motel room and had been following it ever since. They were coming up on a dirt road that had been overrun by tall grass that led off into an embankment from the passenger side of the road.

"Is it possible that leads to it?" Sable asked, pointing it out.

"More than possible."

Glancing around him in all directions Kahner saw there was no one else around. Turning abruptly onto the uneven, unmarked patch of road, he drove the car along as it wound around far back away from the road to a shaded part of the small pond. It was hard to see as it was almost completely circled by trees. Stopping the car, he got out, darting his eyes across the pond, hoping it was deeper than it appeared.

"All right, this is our stop. Everyone out!"

Clambering out of the vehicle, Lisa closed her book on her finger to mark her spot. "Are we having a picnic or something?" she asked, peering at her curiously. Her expression mirrored her mother's. Kahner wondered briefly if she'd grow up to look just like her mother, for according to Sable, the girls long untamable hair was the same dark brown as her mothers had been before it was dyed caramel then black. He noted there wasn't as much of her father Lionel in her, as there was with the boys. He suspected for Lisa's sake that had been a good thing.

"Nope," he said. Dragging all the bags from the car Kahner made sure to pocket his phone then turned the keys in the ignition to neutral. Opening the driver's side door, he began steering and pushing the car toward the pond. He knew he didn't need to take the time to wipe the vehicle down since their prints would wash away from the presence of the pond water.

"What are you doing?" Sable shrieked, looking dumbstruck as she watched him shoving the car towards the edge of the pond. He looked like he was trying to dump the vehicle into the water.

"What does it look like?" he grunted, continuing to shove the vehicle forward.

"Mama, is Daddy Kahner trying to sink the car?" Lisa asked suddenly in awe, while Jordan and Adam started hooting and hollering next to her.

"It sure looks like it," Sable responded dryly. "And that man is not your daddy," she corrected her.

"Better him for a daddy then a drug lord named Lionel Radford," Lisa spat, shocking her mother. "Besides, he told us while you were gone to start calling him Daddy Kahner." Spinning about she stalked away. Dropping down into the grass near a patch of flowers, she sat staring out across the pond angrily, still holding her book in hand.

"Let her be, Sable," Kahner called. The Chevy Lumina began sinking into the water in front of them. He'd stepped into the water to push it out even further into the pond, hoping it would sink faster. Having overheard the conversation, he understood the girl's struggle, knowing full well some of the imagery left from the memory of when her father had beaten her mother was still ever present in her mind. He stood briefly watching the car until it finally began sinking. After a time, he turned and sloshed his way out of the pond, his pants wet up to his hips. He knew he'd need to change again and was glad he had at least one more, dry pair of jeans to wear.

Grabbing up his bag he spied a grouping of brush and trees off to the side of the pond. Pulling his phone from his pocket, he headed in that direction.

"Where are you going? And how exactly do you expect to get around now that you've sunk our only form of transportation?" Sable called after him as he continued to stroll away.

His back to her, he lifted his phone in the air and waved it over his head. "No worries, Sable. Our ride will be here just after about noon."

"Noon?" Sable exclaimed incredulously. "What if it rains? And what are we supposed to eat?"

Turning around Kahner continued to walk backwards, spying the box of doughnuts in her arms. "Not calling for rain today. Besides, you can always have a long-john." Eyes glimmering as he grinned at her while walking backwards, he chuckled at her wide-eyed horrified expression.

She was so cute when she got angry.

- - -

"If he's family, then what does this mean? Is Kahner RavenCroft your real name then?" Sable was extremely anxious. They were apparently being picked up off the side of the road by the man in the Sheriff's uniform.

"Yes." Kahner's tone was clipped, his expression blank.

"Is he for real? I mean, you're a real Sheriff?" Sable's brow furrowed in confusion. She turned her attention from the man in the Sheriff's uniform to the man standing next to the cruiser door. The Sheriff in question had been introduced by Kahner as his brother, Kalturek RavenCroft. Sable hadn't been surprised, considering the man looked identical to Kahner. It would seem his identity as Agent Toni Starck had all been a ruse. The question in her mind now was, why? What would possess a man to assume a new name to work in a government agency like the CIA?

Confused and a little more than frightened at having been picked up by a Loveland County Sheriff, regardless of his familial link to Kahner, Sable was trying hard not to panic. She couldn't quite figure out what was going on and where Kahner was taking her and her children.

Stepping from the cruiser Kalturek waved bags of burgers and fries in his hand and proceeded to apologize for being over an hour late. Explaining that he'd been held up by a speeder who had turned out to have a warrant for his arrest, he greeted his brother with a smile. Then, rapping Kahner on the head, he handed over the food to the waiting kids.

"You do realize I'm not supposed to be taking this cruiser across state lines for *any* reason?" The man's tone was peevish.

"We're only a couple miles south of the Colorado state line." Kahner's expression was all of innocence.

"So not the point and you *know* it. I, of all people, have no business breaking this kind of rule. It sets a bad precedent for my deputies. Why did I absolutely have to pick you up here?"

"Because I needed to dump the car on this side of the state line and that pond there was the best place to do that where it wouldn't be found for a very long time. Besides, what's the big deal? It's only a couple miles."

"The big deal is that I could get in a lot of trouble for crossing state lines with a cruiser. I happen to like being the elected Sheriff of Loveland County. I'd rather not lose the position over something so minute and stupid as this."

"Then I guess we'd better get going rather than standing around here yapping, wouldn't you say?"

Kalturek scowled at his brother, making an unintelligible sound in the back of his throat. "By the way, Dad says you're grounded."

"Right" Kahner responded with a sardonic smile.

They both grinned at each other than hugged. Backing away self-consciously, when they realized Sable was watching them carefully, they both shook hands in their age-old secret greeting.

"He also says to stop scaring the shit out of him."

"Whatever."

"My brother, always a man of so few words."

"That's because you'd never shut up," Kahner said under his breath, though loud enough to hear.

Hauling the bags into the cruiser Kalturek gestured for the kids to get in. Clambering into the back seat excitedly, they each shoved their hands into the bag for a cheeseburger and fries hungrily, while eyeing the two identical men curiously.

"No, really, Kahner. His temper is burning over this one for some reason. Who are they anyway?" Kalturek asked, gesturing toward Sable and the children. The two men were talking about her, right in front of her, and it was making her mad.

"Better left untold. As far as everyone's concerned she's Sable Kryder-my fiancée. I'll be adopting her kids."

"Really?" Kalturek said in surprise. He noted Sable's startled gaze towards Kahner when he spun around. Taking the woman in front of him into careful consideration Kalturek also noticed her beautiful soft brown eyes. Her black hair looked slightly unnatural against her skin for some reason, but aside from that, she was very beautiful.

"Seems congratulations are in order."

Kalturek extended his hand toward her in a cordial greeting. His pale blue eyes, identical to his brothers, squinted in the early afternoon sun.

"You congratulate people who've been given a death sentence?" Sable said. Then she mumbled under her breath while giving Kahner a look that could kill. "Besides, it's the first I've heard of this."

Bursting out laughing, Kalturek turned toward his brother, missing her mumbled words. "Feisty one, isn't she?" He winked as he grinned. Then his face sobered suddenly. "Which reminds me; speaking of death sentences..."

"Not now," Kahner ground out dangerously. He'd nodded towards the children in the back seat of the car, who were hungrily munching on their French fries while watching the adults intently.

Stalking around the vehicle toward the other cruiser door, Sable moved to get in while gesturing toward Kahner rudely. "You both look the same. You two also got the same sweet-talking, genteel personality?"

Barking aloud, Kalturek laughed and got into the cruiser, while Kahner moved around to the front passenger seat. He grinned back at her.

"Nope. I'm the dashing debonair gentlemanly sort myself," Kalturek called. "I got chocolate shakes up here for everyone." Reaching around and through the lowered patrol windows, he handed them over to the eagerly awaiting hands.

"Mama, I left my book," Lisa exclaimed suddenly.

Head slumping forward, Sable banged it on the cage in front of them, which separated the Sheriff's deputies from their prisoners in the back seat. Feeling like a bit of a prisoner herself, Sable extricated herself from the cruiser and headed quickly for the patch of flowers her daughter had been sitting near. Before she was out of earshot she managed to catch Kalturek's last words as he'd turned towards his brother.

"No, but seriously, Kahner. Does she know Dad's planning to kill her?"

Whipping her head around, Sable gasped in surprise as she stared back at the two men sitting in the front seat. They had clearly been speaking, for they were staring at each other, but their lips didn't seem to move. Shaking her head to clear it, Sable listened as they continued to callously speak about her impending demise. Knowing now that Kahner's brother Kalturek was the actual head Sheriff of Loveland County Colorado, she found the blatant conversation both disturbing and unsettling, especially in front of her children. Seeing

Kahner hadn't noticed her glance back at them, she hastily turned away, believing neither man knew she had overheard.

Kahner reached for his sandwiches.

At the same time, Kalturek was observing the woman now walking away from them with a suspicious gaze. He then smacked the take-out bag next to him shut. Head twisting back around, he glared at his brother.

"Really? You had to sleep with her?" Kalturek thought silently. He continued to glare at his brother out of the corner of his eye as he snatched the bag away from Kahner's grasping hands.

"Drop it Kalturek," Kahner retorted under his breath. "Give me my damn sandwiches. You were late, and I'm hungry." He shot a look towards Sable's departing figure. Fully aware she was panicking; he was trying to figure out the best way to alleviate her anxiety without saying too much just yet. The decision he'd made just that morning where Sable and her children were concerned still needed to be approved by his father Bastion.

"You didn't glove it, did you?" Kalturek accused with another silent thought. He took a large bite out of one of his sandwiches while continuing to hold his brother's hostage until he got his answers.

Snatching the bag away from Kalturek roughly, Kahner snarled.

"It's none of your business." Then thinking better of his brother's unorthodox and highly intrusive question, he shifted his gaze back and forth between Sable and Kalturek curiously. "Wait a minute, why are you asking?"

Exhaling deeply Kalturek set his sandwich down and grabbed a French fry. "Because I'm pretty sure she heard what we were thinking just now about Dad killing her off." Thinking his words rather than speaking them, he turned his head and watched Sable return from the field of flowers with a book in hand. Stumbling slightly on her trek back to the car she righted herself than limped the rest of the way.

"Impossible," Kahner said aloud causing the children in the back seat to look at him. Realizing he was responding to statements and questions they couldn't hear, Kahner stopped responding verbally. Kalturek and Kahner had always had a particularly strong link which allowed them to communicate without speaking, for they could hear each other's thoughts.

"We both know full well that anything is possible."

"No, it's impossible because it just happened early this morning. It would be too soon." He paused thoughtfully. "Wouldn't it?"

Shrugging, Kalturek settled back in his seat and started the engine. "Don't know what to tell you. The look on her face a moment ago makes me wonder."

Casting a look in her direction, they both noted she was nearly back to the vehicle. Jerking his head in her direction Kalturek silently posed another question.

"What's she thinking right now?"

Kalturek could only hear his brother's thoughts because of their link. Reading minds wasn't his gift. His ability had always been seeing a kind of aura around people; just then she'd been pulsing between black and white.

Kahner eyed her intently. The closer Sable came to the vehicle the easier it was for him to read her thoughts.

"He has a whole other life," she was thinking. "Why would he do that? And why would he take up a new identity if he was really working for the CIA?" Then she sopped suddenly, and Kahner could hear another disturbing thought pop in her head.

"Oh, my God, what if he's married? Is he? Is Kahner married?" Sable bit her lip worriedly, her hand reaching toward the missing pendant that used to hang around her neck.

Frowning, Kahner unwrapped his sandwich and called out to her before taking a bite. "Rest assured, Sable, I'm not married."

Giving him a startled look, Sable gaped.

Feeling a hand smack against his side Kahner growled at his brother. "Stop it, Kalturek. Get in the car, Sable. My brother's not wrong, we need to get moving."

Crawling into the back seat, she wedged herself between her boys as she traded her daughter the book for a cheeseburger from their bag.

"Dad's going to kill you when he finds out about her," Kalturek thought, shifting a suspicious sideways glance at his brother.

Distracted, Sable began mumbling irritably. "Wish you guys would stop talking about me like that."

"Mama, no one's talking about you," Lisa said in confusion, peering between the men in the front seat and her mother curiously.

Kalturek and Kahner turned and stared at each other as though in silent conversation, then glanced back at Sable from the front seat of the cruiser. She realized neither of them must have said a word, causing her heart to leap in her chest. What was going on? Was she going crazy?

"Do you have kids, Kahner?" Sable asked, attempting to dispel the awkwardness. Her breathing slowed as her heart raced. From the look Kahner gave her, she wished she hadn't asked.

"No," Kahner said shortly then turned away. He stared out the windshield, ignoring the heated reproachful gaze of the man next to him. Both men were careful to school their thoughts, not wanting to alarm her further.

Glancing back at her through the rearview mirror Kalturek noticed her expression. "If it's any consolation, it's a sore subject for him," he offered gently, trying to ease her obvious anxiety.

Startled, Sable couldn't help but ask, "Why? How so?"

Both men exchanged looks once again, then Kahner appeared to shoot Kalturek a kind of warning look.

Putting the cruiser in motion, Kalturek guided it back onto the road. He knew better than to say anything further where that issue was concerned. "It just is."

Chapter 12

"Are you absolutely sure about this?" Kalturek snuck another look in the rear-view mirror. Sable and her children had fallen asleep in the back seat of his patrol car.

Kahner scowled. "Just do it." He understood his brother's anxiety all too well but was trying hard not to let on that he was just as worried. The last time someone other than a RavenCroft had crossed into their land, was the day his sister, Synedra, had gotten married to Nathan Kayme and it had been out of necessity for the wedding itself. The feathered inhabitants who had been utilizing the valley as their sanctuary for hundreds of years, had been most disagreeable to his presence until shortly after Nathan and Synedra had officially wed. How the creatures were capable of discerning when an individual had become part of the family or not was unclear to them. The running theory was that they had a kind of auric sight like Kalturek's, which allowed them to see an aura change taking place. Their wedding pictures could attest to the difficulties his new brother-in-law had endured prior to the ceremony. He had band-aids everywhere and holes in his suit.

No doubt, his father would be upset to find out he was bringing Sable and her children to the ranch before having any kind of arrangement with her. But he really had no choice.

Whistling softly, Kalturek gave in to the inevitable and turned off the main road onto a dirt path. They'd been arguing silently back and forth over whether or not taking them into the valley was even a good idea or not.

"All right," he grudgingly agreed. "It's your funeral."

"You *are* the one driving, you know. So it won't be all on me."

"Huh, uh. You don't get to put me in the middle. This is all on you. You're the eldest so I have no choice but to do what I'm told."

Ignoring his brother, Kahner looked out the window. He disliked being reminded of his position within the family. He, Kalturek, and Kalabernus were triplets so they were the same age. But he was the first to be born, which made him head of the, for lack of a better word, clan.

"We'll watch their response carefully as we head into the valley, and I'll deal with his wrath as it comes."

Kalturek laughed. They both rolled their eyes and grinned at each other, unable to squelch the slight bit of irony in his statement.

From the back seat, Sable had awakened from her dozing state against the cruisers windshield at the sound of the men's voices. The exchange had seemed odd to her. She got the feeling Kahner was doing something he shouldn't be doing. Lifting her head away from the windshield she blinked rapidly, trying to get her bearings. She took in their surroundings as they drove along the dirt path. If they hadn't been already driving on it, she likely wouldn't have known it was there. One minute the path appeared to be covered in bramble and brush no normal vehicle would ever be able to drive through, the next the foliage would recede from the center and back off to the sides of the road as they progressed, as if it simply disappeared into thin air. She blinked again several times in succession to make sure she was seeing things clearly. Was it possible she was still dreaming or were her eyes playing tricks on her?

"She's awake." She heard Kalturek grumble from the driver's seat.

Kahner grimaced, glancing back at Sable briefly. He supposed it was inevitable. He wondered briefly what she was seeing other than the forest surrounding them. He was aware it might be different for those who weren't gifted. Then again...

Opting to stay quiet since she still felt groggy from her nap, Sable adjusted in her seat, anxious to be out of the cramped quarters of the car. She was so tired of being cooped up in vehicles. Her movements disturbed her daughter sitting next to her. All three of her children had fallen asleep during the long drive as well. She peered down at her watch. Small wonder. They'd been driving for over three and a half hours.

The children began to stir as the patrol car drove slowly along the path. Kalturek was clearly attempting to avoid any deer or critters that might dart across the dirt road for they were surrounded by trees and brush on all sides. Sunlight could barely find its way through the densely packed trees. It made it seem darker out then what it should be for the time of day, which was starting to make Sable nervous. Would she be able to find her way out if she had to?

Taking another look around her, she looked back through the rear windshield. The dirt road looked like it was disappearing as soon as they passed over it. How was that even possible? She realized the likelihood of getting lost was high if she was unable to even see the road.

"Now that you're all awake I have a little piece of advice for everyone," Kalturek said loudly as he turned down the radio. "Is everyone listening? Do I have your attention?" He waited for them all to nod in unison. "Good. Do not, under any circumstances, wander off on your own – any of you. Not even in pairs. You *will* get lost in this valley. I cannot guarantee we'd be able to find you in time."

"In time for what?" Lisa asked next to her, before her mother could.

Sunlight slammed into their faces unexpectedly, forcing them to close their eyes and peer away briefly. They'd pulled into a bit of a clearing. Before Kalturek was able to respond, a swarm of black birds pelted across the sky in front of the vehicle, forcing him to creep along even slower. The birds were large and loud, cawing as they flew in tandem. The waving ribbon of black creatures swooped before them into the meadow clearing, causing the children to exclaim first in fright then in awe. There were hundreds of them. Quite possibly over a thousand. They all suddenly plummeted toward the ground, landing together as one. Their black heads, beaks, legs and feathers gleamed in the sunlight as they began searching and pecking among the grass.

It took a minute before Sable finally realized what they were. Their tails had been wedge shaped while in flight which could only mean... "Are those..."

"-Ravens." Kahner confirmed.

"There's so many of them," Jordan cried.

"That was so cool," Adam said, giving Lisa cause to shake her head.

"Only *you* would think that was cool. It scared the crap out of *me*. Ugh, ravens. How creepy."

"How is it there are so many of them together like this?" Sable never imagined ravens would fly in swarming packs like that.

"This valley is, you could say...sort of a haven for ravens." Kalturek said in answer. He exchanged looks with his brother. "Though...our father runs a horse ranch here. As long as you don't bother them, they won't bother you."

"Usually."

Kahner's murmured response was barely audible. Sable wasn't sure she wanted to know what that meant. She gazed back out over the field of ravens blackening the grass as they drove by them. They were about to pass through the clearing back into a section of forest when suddenly the ravens erupted as one from the grass and flew away, tunneling through the cavernous path they were about to enter.

Heart thundering in her chest, Sable's mouth went dry. Why did she get the feeling that was a bad omen?

As the cruiser crossed over into the forest again Sable found herself grabbing for her ears. There was a popping sensation and sound that made her feel like a needle had just punctured a hole in the vacuum of space. It was a ridiculous analogy but she couldn't come up with a better one. She noticed her children had the same response. Finally able to remove their hands from their ears, they each rolled their jaw around as if trying to make their ears pop.

"You guys too, eh?" she asked her children, noticing that it appeared Kalturek and Kahner had been unaffected. All three of her kids nodded. "That was weird, wasn't it? I wonder what caused it."

The two men in the front seat didn't say a word but shifted uneasily in unison. They were officially in for it now.

Ten minutes later, Sable was starting to get antsy. They were still driving slowly along the forest path and it didn't seem to end. On either side of her, she could see raven upon raven perched in the branches of the trees nearby. She knew it was absurd but she got the distinct impression they were following the vehicles progression through the forest. The notion made her uneasy.

"Geez, Kahner. How long is this stretch?" she finally asked.

He shrugged. "We're about there."

Even as he said it, Kalturek pulled the vehicle out of the tunnel of trees into a vast clearing. Several football fields before them was a large log ranch home, set before a row of trees. It looked like the house and horse barns were nestled within a very large valley for they were surrounded by mountains on all sides. Above the tree line she could see the Rocky Mountains surging up behind the house at a height greater than the rest of them and above that a large school of black ravens swooped and swirled high in the sky over the home. Suddenly they dove, pelting toward the vehicle as if prepared to attack. A startled cry escaped Sable's lips as she ducked unnecessarily within the vehicle. The swarm of birds flew over and past them, back through the tunnel of trees, leaving a few stragglers behind in the meadow near the house. There were several still perched on eaves of the house as well, as if awaiting their arrival.

"This could get interesting." Kalturek eyed the giant raven sitting on the porch. It plumed its wings angrily at them as if daring them to proceed then tucked them back into its sides. The regal posture and black disdain filled eyes glared at them accusingly. Kalturek gave his brother a questioning look. The raven king, as they not so affectionately called him, had taken post on their porch which usually did not bode well.

"It'll be fine."

Kahner's response didn't sound anywhere near as sure as Sable would have liked. Or Kalturek, from all appearances. What exactly was he getting her into?

Chapter 13

They arrived at the RavenCroft horse ranch four hours after having been picked up by Kalturek. The shock of the swarming ravens dissipated as the cruiser made its way toward the house. The view of the sprawling ranch and multiple horse barns had Sable's children exclaiming with excitement.

At a second glance, Sable noted the main house had been constructed in the typical log cabin style and it appeared to have been added onto over the years. It had the look and feel of an immense, grand winter vacation home rather than a ranch house attached to a horse ranching business. About fifty yards from the main house they could easily view four horse barns and a half-dozen horse corals. The living quarters for the handful of ranch hands they kept on retainer to work and tend to the horses were set a short distance back from the barns.

"Is this where we're staying tonight?" Jordan asked hopefully, his gaze shifting excitedly between the ranch house and the horse corals where a couple men were in the middle of training an appaloosa.

Responding in the affirmative, Kahner nodded his head. Squaring his shoulders for the inevitable stand-off with his father, he helped everyone from the cruiser. The ravens on the eaves and the one on the porch flew away the instant the doors creaked open. Both the RavenCroft men gave a relieved sigh.

After assisting in carrying their bags up to the front porch, Kalturek waved in acknowledgement toward his father's foreman standing near the corals and attempted a hasty retreat.

"Where do you think you're going?" Kahner halted his brother with a hand to the shoulder. He noted the foreman's curious gaze at the sight of him home after so many years.

"Home. Don't want to keep Stephanie waiting."

"I thought you were... "

"I haven't lived at the ranch house since Stephanie and I got married eight years ago. You know that."

"Right." Kahner winced. Digging the heel of his shoe into the porch he became agitated. "Guess I just thought..."

"Thought what? That I was gonna stick around and help you wade through this?" Kalturek gestured toward Sable and her children waiting on the porch. A loud barking laugh emanated from his throat. "No way. You're on your own."

"Feeling the love here."

"No worries. You won't be alone here with Dad."

"I thought everyone had their own place now."

"Everyone but Kalabernus."

"Last I heard he was living in the cabin Dad had built for him," Kahner said, more than a little surprised at the news.

Kalturek sighed, a grim expression crossing his handsome features. "Let's just say it didn't work out so well. So, Dad's been renting it for him."

"What happened?" Kahner's sharp inquiry gained Sable's attention, making her wonder what she'd missed.

Turning back towards his brother Kalturek responded. "I need to give you fair warning here. Kalabernus has gotten worse. I don't think it likely he's ever going to be able to leave this house and live alone again."

Edgy, Kahner gave the children a sideways glance, ignoring Sable's concerned gaze. "Is it safe for the children to be here?" he thought silently, locking gazes with his brother." Sensing Sable flinch both men cast a glance her direction.

Sable looked visibly spooked. Inching closer to her children they watched her fidget as she looked away anxiously.

Brows raised Kalturek exhaled then descended the stairs. "One problem at a time. Deal with this first, then you can determine that. I don't think it'll be too much of an issue but…"

Giving a short nod of understanding, Kahner opened the front door and herded the children through the door, effectively cutting his brother off. As he closed the door behind him, he watched his brother walk away towards his Sheriff's cruiser, calling out, "good luck!" as he went.

"Fat chance luck is going to save my butt," Kahner grumbled under his breath.

"You can say that again," an irate male voice hollered from behind him.

Walking towards him from the hallway near the kitchen was his father Bastion and his brother Kalabernus. The children's eyes widened at the sight of his brother, the giant of a man lumbering toward them. Three inches taller than the two other men in the room at six feet eight and decidedly brutish in size, the solid build and vast breadth of the man's chest and shoulders startled even Sable.

"Whoa," Sable breathed deeply, not realizing she spoke aloud.

"Whoa is right. The largest of my sons and second born of my triplets, Kalabernus." Bastion gestured toward the brutish man who stepped forward, extending his hand.

"Triplets? Wait a minute, you're a triplet, Kahner?" Sable inquired in surprise, allowing her hand to be dwarfed within the man's beefy hand.

"Multiple births tend to run in the family," Kahner responded nonchalantly.

"And you are?" Kalabernus spoke with a deep smooth voice. Releasing her small hand, he peered down appreciatively at the woman in the entryway.

Tongue tied, Sable didn't speak initially. Though his features were quite similar, he was mind-numbingly gorgeous in comparison to his brothers. Yet there was something about him that was unsettling.

She shivered, then shaking her head as though to clear it, she finally replied. "My name is Kalysta … wait. Sorry. Sable. My name is Sable Kryder." Blushing profusely at her blunder, she wanted to crawl into a hole at the look Bastion gave her.

"We'll want to get better at that, now won't we?" Bastion levelled a cool gaze upon the woman as though attempting to size her up. "Wouldn't want any unwanted, unexpected visitors, now would we?" His caustic manner and aggressive stance immediately put Sable on the defensive.

"I'll take your bags for you and take your kids up to their rooms," Kalabernus offered quickly, sensing it might be a good idea to remove the children from the impending explosion. Hastily taking up all the bags, including Kahner's, he gestured for the children to follow up the entryway staircase.

"Mama?" Lisa questioned nervously, intimidated by the man's size, good looks, and dark countenance.

"Go ahead, Honey. It's okay. Mama will be just downstairs."

"There's a television and game system in each room," Kalabernus called as he ascended the stairs, attempting to entice the children.

Squealing with excitement, they followed him, soon disappearing down the upstairs hallway.

"Now that tender ears are no longer present I trust we can get to the heart of the matter," Bastion said.

"Look, Dad…"

"Does she know? Have you told her yet?" Bastion inquired on a silent thought. He stared intently at his son, his anger threatening to spill forth into words.

"Do I know what?" Sable demanded, gaining Bastion's startled glance. Her face had been turned toward her children, watching them intently as they disappeared upstairs. Turning back toward the men who were cautiously watching her, she gave them a fierce look. "Are you referring to my imminent demise?" Sable asked, noting Bastion's jaw clench. "Because from what I gather from your son, Kalturek, you intend to kill me for some reason," she stated boldly.

Becoming increasingly anxious at their lack of response and intent gaze Sable began to ramble nervously, unable to stop herself. The overwhelming desire to flee washed over her but she stood her ground. "I don't know who you think you are. For that matter, I don't even know who you are. But where I come from, a person usually has a good reason for wanting to kill someone. I've done absolutely nothing to you to warrant such dislike. How dare you threaten me. How dare you threaten to orphan my children…"

Both annoyed and amused, Bastion halted her tirade. "Enough. I'm afraid your death is essential regardless of your opinion on the matter." Moving towards her Bastion towered over her, noting her pallor had become drawn, and surprisingly pale considering her tanned skin tone, out of fear.

Though three inches shorter than Kalabernus, Bastion made a formidable and imposing figure himself, what with his own breadth and size. Unable to control herself, Sable couldn't help but think she was surrounded by giants.

Kahner chuckled upon overhearing her thought, then approached his father. He couldn't blame Sable for thinking that, for he and Kalturek matched their father in height.

"Dad, this really isn't necessary."

"What are your intentions towards this woman, Kahner?" Bastioned asked shortly, giving Sable a calculating stare.

"We'll have the ceremony Friday," he insisted quickly. He sounded as though he were anxious to appease his father.

Briefly glancing at his son, Bastion's gaze roamed over Sable once again. "Damn right you will. Geez, Kahner, what were you thinking?" Bastion bellowed. "She knows too much now. *They* know too much now," he emphasized as he continued to holler, pointing in the direction the children had disappeared.

Sable shivered once again. The man appeared to be maybe fifty, yet she sensed somehow that he might be older. His domineering erect posture and glowering pale blue eyes, so like his sons, made it obvious he was rarely questioned or argued with.

"I had no choice."

"You always have a choice. Whether you made a good one remains to be seen," Bastion countered heatedly. He paced before the two of them in the entryway, his booted feet clomping loudly against the worn wooden floor.

Inhaling deeply, Kahner's lips thinned as he clenched his teeth. A muscle near his jaw jumped, the only sign that his carefully composed and calm cool façade was waning.

"There's a mole within the agency."

Bastion halted abruptly. Whirling around, he faced his son.

"Who?"

"Ripley Braddock."

The sharp intake of breath was the only sign Bastion registered the name, though he noted Sable's head jerk towards Kahner in alarm.

"How did you know it was Ripley Braddock?"

"We'll get into that later, Sable."

"She doesn't know yet. Does she?" Bastion inquired. Seeing his son's slight headshake he continued. "How did you learn of this? And where's your proof?"

"I'm not sure it's safe to say."

"You're not sure…" Bastion scoffed and then laughed. "Oh, well, he's not sure it's safe," he shouted, glancing toward Sable with menace in his eye. "Who is she, Kahner, and why have you brought her here? Do you realize the danger you've placed the entire family in, by bringing her here? Have you any comprehension of the precarious and dangerous position you've placed her and her children in?"

"What is he talking about, Kahner?" Sable's voice rose as she spoke. Frightened by his line of questioning, Sable felt a vice grip the heart wildly beating in her chest.

"I will explain everything later," Kahner said hastily. He turned back to his father. "And as for who she is and where she comes from; you of all people know it's best that I not say." He gave Bastion a meaningful look, compelling him to understand with his eyes. A strangled sound escaped his father's thinning lips. Kahner had never seen such a horrified look cross his face.

Rolling his eyes heavenward Bastion fisted his hands together at his sides.

"Blast it all, Kahner! Are you telling me you brought work home with you?" Bastion roared, advancing on his son.

Refusing to allow his father to intimidate him, Kahner didn't back down. "I had no choice," he insisted.

"You had no choice? You keep saying you had no choice. *Every* man has a choice. Oh, God, Kahner!" Raking his hands through his salt and pepper colored hair, Bastion began pacing once again, his movements quicker than moments before. Spinning around suddenly, he pointed toward Sable.

"Who are you really?" Bastion demanded, tempering his anger, though his voice remained chilled. He knew that frightening her wouldn't get him the answers he sought.

Sable peered back and forth between the two men, unsure of what to do. Making a hasty decision she answered honestly. "Kalysta Radford."

"Kalysta Radford," Bastion said coldly, the blood in his veins turning to ice, "I know that name. She was married to Lionel Radford – brother to Kobi Radford – the drug cartel kingpin with business dealings in over five different countries. She died three days ago along with her three children."

Stunned at his knowledge Sable inquired, "How do you know that?"

Sighing in resignation Kahner's shoulders drooped in defeat, ignoring her question for the moment. "Yes, Dad, that's what I've been trying to tell you. You needn't kill her because I already have."

The words echoed in the entryway. He glanced suddenly towards Sable, understanding dawned on him. "I already killed you," Kahner repeated, recalling the story her children had told him. Had fate brought the two of them together somehow?

Eyes wide in shock, Sable swallowed hard. The revelation that the words of her angel from many years before had come true was astounding. What did this mean? Breathing heavily, she clasped her hand against her chest desperately attempting to gain comfort from the missing elk tooth necklace to no avail.

"It's true. I'm thought to be dead now, aren't I? But I'm still alive," she whimpered. Kahner had explained to her as they'd travelled through Mexico, how he and Agent Pegueros had set things up before picking her up at Lionel and Kobi's office building, to make it appear she and the children died in a plane crash while trying to escape.

Closing her eyes on a wave of nausea, Sable felt faint as she opened them. Suddenly feeling disoriented, she stumbled as the shadowy blackness enveloped her.

Barely catching her before she fell, Kahner adjusted his hold until he had her in a more secure position in his arms. "Whoa, Sable. What's the matter with you?"

"She fainted *obviously*," Bastion snorted in disgust. "Let me guess; this woman is how you knew the mole was Ripley Braddock. Am I right?" His vast intellect was evident in his eyes. But that wasn't the only thing Kahner could see, for the pieces were falling into place within his mind, forming the conclusion he wasn't sure his father should know. Yet somehow in that same instant, he knew Bastion needed to know the truth.

"Yes, and she has proof."

"Where? Have you seen this so-called proof? Is it for real?" Bastion demanded to know.

"It's in my bag. She showed it to me at our first stop in Mexico. We'll want to get the documents and recording in the safe right away."

"But you didn't find out until after you pulled her and was about to place her in witness protection, did you?"

"You would be correct in your theory."

A thoughtful expression replaced the angry visage from moments before. "Kahner, what prompted your desire to disappear with her? You could have relocated her outside of WITSEC but instead, you came home? Why?"

Setting Sable gently down on the couch, Kahner covered her with a blanket, tucking it around her. He then peered back at his father with a troubled expression.

"The last agent I worked with made the statement that I reminded him of someone else he knew. Someone he'd worked with undercover within the agency."

"And this was troubling why?"

"Because it's not the first time an agent has said this to me. Others have made the same statement."

Becoming alarmed Bastion stared at his son. "Did this last man say who…?"

"Franc Kastle."

Stunned, Bastion gaped, speechless for the first time in over twenty years. "The Punisher?" Bastion croaked.

Only slightly alarmed by his father's stricken response, Kahner had a bad feeling he knew why. Clearing his throat, he continued.

"I think we both know what that likely means."

"Yes. Yes, this changes everything, Kahner. No wonder you brought her home with you. She's not safe anywhere right now."

Silence fell between them as they both stared down at the woman resting in her unconscious state.

"I'm afraid there's more."

"More? Kahner, the woman you brought home is the supposedly deceased estranged wife of Lionel Radford who happens to know, and have proof mind you, that Ripley Braddock, a high-ranking official within the CIA is in his pocket! Additionally, your cover may have been compromised by a potential cousin, which may invariably one day bring the government to our doorstep looking for our gifted family. What more could there possibly…?"

"Kalturek and I think she might be pregnant."

Groaning in understanding at what his son was telling him, Bastion exploded once again. "For the love of God, Kahner! You had to sleep with Lionel Radford's wife?"

"Technically speaking she's not his wife anymore."

"And technically speaking you had sex with a dead woman!" Bastion snapped. "You couldn't have worn a glove?"

"It wasn't exactly planned…"

"When?"

"This morning actually," Kahner responded with a silly grin.

Whacking at his son's arm with a nearby magazine Bastion glowered at him. "Wipe that smile off your face, Boy. Now, are you telling me that your encounter with this woman was just this morning?"

"Yup," Kahner responded, only mildly irritated to be called a boy at the age of forty.

"There are already signs?" Bastion queried, more than a little flabbergasted by this news.

"Kalturek caught on first. So, he tested her. And just now…"

"Yeah, I know I saw," Bastion responded in a rush, sounding both cross and tickled all in one. "You're sure she wasn't always gifted? There could be more like us out there after all."

Shaking his head Kahner replied seriously. "She and I have been attached at the hip for nearly four days now. If she were gifted in some way, I'd have noticed it by now. I'm pretty sure this is a new development."

"You're going to need to marry this woman, Kahner. Is she going to be acquiescent to this plan?"

"One way or another I'll convince her," Kahner said vehemently, causing his father to eye him curiously.

"You like her, don't you?" Bastion questioned. Not getting a response Bastion simply harrumphed softly and bobbed his head. "Good then. The marriage should fix everything. Keep everyone safe for both Sable and the children included. But you must tell her, Kahner, and before the wedding Friday. I won't have her marrying into this family without knowing of our powers. It's bad enough she might already be pregnant without having that knowledge first."

"I agree. I don't want a repeat of Eliza any more than you," Kahner said, both hope and worry springing to his eyes. "We need to find out for sure."

"Agreed."

"When is Synedra expected home again?"

"Don't expect to see her or Nathan for another week or so. Or rather, not until Friday now, I guess," Bastion said in answer. It occurred to him everyone should be called home for the ceremony.

"I cannot wait that long. I need Synedra here sooner. I need to know."

"I will call her and the rest of the family now. We'll have a family get together on the premise of your return home and subsequent engagement. But Kahner…, if what you and Kalturek believe is true, then you had better be prepared for a fight when Synedra arrives."

"Wait, why?"

"Kalturek and Stephanie; they've been trying to have children for the past eight years with no success. Drayke and Laynie too. When Stephanie and Laynie find out..."

"All hell is going to break loose." Swearing Kahner groaned, wondering at why the universe had to be so cruel. Why couldn't his brothers have children when without even meaning to, he could?

Chapter 14

That is most definitely a good question. Why can Kahner have children when his siblings can't? Of course, this is going on the assumption at this point that because Sable appears to be able to know what they are thinking, she might possibly be pregnant. One good way to find out for sure before needlessly alarming Sable was to bring his sister, Synedra, home to meet her.

Oh, did I not mention? Synedra can tell when a woman is in the family way just by looking at them.

Obviously, I wasn't kidding when I said things were going to get messy. Because if Sable was with child Kahner now had the added worry that she might make the same decision his first wife, Eliza, had made when she found out. Kahner didn't want history repeating itself; he wanted this child desperately. Somehow, he had to figure out a way to tell Sable about his and his family's abilities without frightening her and then ease her into the notion that she would be experiencing the ability to know people's thoughts throughout her pregnancy. After that, he had to convince her somehow to marry him by Friday.

Did you happen to also catch Bastion's comment? Sable caught it. Now she's panicking and rightfully so. It was more of a question as to whether Kahner knew the dangerous and precarious position he'd placed Sable and her children in just by bringing them there to stay.

Now why would Sable and her kids be in danger in Bastion RavenCroft's home, you wonder?

Clearly, there is still more going on here because even Kalturek left Kahner with a warning if you recall. It had to do with their brother, Kalabernus, for his ability wasn't so much a gift as it was a curse and for whatever the reason lately it had been getting worse.

- - -

"What's the deal with your brother, Kahner?"

Sable glared at the man standing before her.

Just that morning she woke to find Kalabernus watching her from her bedroom doorway. Shutting the door on him she'd showered and changed only to step back into her bedroom and find Kalabernus sitting on her bed, peering around the room anxiously. She thought she overheard him mumbling about shadows at play in the corners of her room. But when Sable asked him what he was talking about, he responded he hadn't said a word.

Then later at lunchtime, she literally ran into Kalabernus coming out of the kitchen. The man had been spying on her as she'd prepared and had lunch with her children. When she offered to make him some lunch, she thought he'd replied that he had already eaten some brain soup for lunch and that it had been quite tasty. When she'd inquired if she'd heard him right, then repeated what he'd said, Kalabernus responded he hadn't said a thing. He then proceeded to ask if she was sure she'd heard him right.

By dinner time that evening, Sable was becoming increasingly paranoid. She couldn't escape the nagging notion that something wasn't quite right in the RavenCroft household. Or was it that something wasn't quite right with her?

The last incident which had sent her nerves to jangling was when Kalabernus had accepted a roll from the basket she'd passed, and then requested that she pass him the pear butter. When she attempted to hand it to him he asked if she was sure he'd been the one to ask for it. Slamming the jar back on the table she'd glowered at him in irritation as he cast a wary gaze around the room. The man seemed jumpy, haunted maybe out of sorts even. It worried her.

"Kahner, I asked you a question."

Sighing almost wearily, Kahner continued to stare out the picture window in the front living room. He'd been staring outside for the past twenty minutes after having started a fire in the hearth.

"What isn't wrong with him?" Kahner thought.

"What does that mean?"

Sable had just come down from putting her children to bed and had decided it was high time to confront him. She needed answers. She needed to know what his plans were for her and her children. And she needed to know if his brother Kalabernus posed a threat to them.

Turning around Kahner faced her. She truly was beautiful, he thought, suspecting she'd probably heard that too. He had not spoken a word, but she was clearly able to read his thoughts. The knowledge she could do this was both exhilarating and frightening to him.

"It means he sees shadows."

His response confused her. "What do you mean by that?" Sable asked warily.

"Just that," Kahner shrugged. "He sees shadows."

"You mean he's touched in the head?"

"No, Sable. I mean, he sees demonic shadows."

Sable stared. He was messing with her. He had to be, she thought.

"I'm not messing with you," Kahner insisted, his expression grim. "It's part of a family secret that I will eventually need to tell you about. But in the interest of safety for the children, you need to know this."

"You're kidding me with this, right?" Clearly, he'd somehow ascertained what she had been thinking.

"I only wish I was. But that conversation is for another day. Right now, we need to talk about Friday."

"Why? What happens Friday?"

The night before, Kahner and his father had determined they'd need to share the information she needed to know in bits and pieces or they might overwhelm her. Or worse, frighten her away.

"Sable, I know we don't always see eye to eye on things."

"You can say that again," Sable scoffed, and then softly chuckled.

Moving toward the couch he sat down next to her. Surprising her, he took her hands in his and looked her square in the eye.

Sable's pulse quickened at his touch. He had that effect on her. More than she cared to admit.

"That said, I think we both can agree that my intentions have always been toward keeping you and your children safe. Would you agree?"

Gazing at him thoughtfully Sable tilted her head.

"Yes," she responded slowly. Somehow, she just knew she wasn't going to like what he was about to say.

Accepting her answer, he nodded briefly and continued. "Okay, so here's the plan. When you overheard me tell my brother Kalturek that we were engaged, and that I'd be adopting your children, I wasn't kidding. Friday we'll be getting married." Kahner inhaled sharply, awaiting her response with not but a little bit of anxiety.

Sable peered up at Kahner through her long lashes in disbelief. "You're serious with this?" she exclaimed, her voice breathy. She was unable to explain the little thrill of pleasure that had shot through her at his words.

"Dead serious. It's the only way I know of, to protect you and the kids fully. I can keep you safe. You'll never have to worry about Lionel finding you here in the valley."

For a moment Sable sat in silence. Her thought process struggled to make sense of what he was saying. A half-smile played on her lips and she found herself expelling a soft breath in nervous amusement.

"Oh, come on, Kahner," she said finally, her voice shaky as she spoke. "You cannot tell me that there isn't another solution…."

"I can relocate you elsewhere," Kahner stated automatically. "You would be alone, a single mother of three children, attempting to make it on your own." Seeing she was about to speak in her defense, Kahner raised his hand in front of her to shush her. "And being an independent woman, I've no doubt that you could do it. That said, there is a chance you'd be found out, and by not placing you somewhere through WITSEC you would have no protection if that happened."

Sable stopped suddenly.

"What do you think is going to happen if Lionel and Kobi were to ever discover Agent Pegueros ruse to make you and your children appear dead was all a sham?" he asked.

Cringing, Sable shivered violently, knowing full well what they would do. "It won't be just Lionel coming after me. Kobi will want my head too. They'll both start looking for me. They won't stop until they find and kill me."

"Exactly. Look, I went through all those, as you put it, 'painstakingly annoying efforts' to prevent them from ever finding you for a reason. But here's the thing. I also must consider every variable. And knowing that Ripley Braddock is in Kobi's pocket doesn't help. So, I cannot use normal channels to get you new identification. What I've given you so far will only work for so long. You need a permanent solution. And if it would happen, where they'd come after you, as I suspect they already have, then they'll be looking for what you are now; a mother with three children."

"I see, but not a married woman with three kids. Right?"

"Yes."

"So, your only reason for marrying me and adopting them is to protect me and my kids?"

"I won't lie. I have other ulterior motives now," Kahner responded evenly, leaving it at that. His gaze roamed appreciatively down the length of her before returning to her face. He shifted in his seat.

Becoming suspicious, Sable's gaze narrowed on him. "What exactly are we talking here? Are your reasons simply sexual or is there something else going on?"

Sable's eyes twinkled.

Clearly, she had noticed his semi-aroused state.

Agitated, Kahner cleared his throat before responding. More than ever, he was frustrated by his family's inherited trait. He struggled to reign in his insatiable desire for intimacy with the beauty before him. Deciding it wouldn't hurt to broach that subject with her, he leaned forward. The feel of her soft skin within his hand incited within him a carnal desire to throw her to the floor and ravish her.

"That does bring up a question I have."

Exasperated by his lack of response, Sable sighed heavily. "Sure, why not? I'll answer your question but only if you agree to finally answer some of mine."

The corners of Kahner's mouth lifted with an amused smile. Chuckling softly, he rubbed his forefinger in a circular pattern within the palm of her hand.

Inhaling tremulously at his touch Sable closed her eyes briefly then opened them. She noted he had been watching her reaction to his touch and it seemed to please him. Jerking her hand away self-consciously, Sable shook it lightly, attempting to dispel the tingling sensation she was experiencing.

"In the end, Sable, the decision is up to you. I cannot force you to do anything you do not want to. I can merely advise you of the best course."

"The best course being…"

"To marry me on Friday."

"Right." Frowning, Sable gazed into his handsome face, marveling once again at the similar appearance he shared with his father, Bastion. "That's not really a question. Unless…, is this your way of trying to ask me to marry you?"

Groaning, Kahner laughed. "What I'm trying to ask, in my albeit awkward fashion is this; should we marry would you be averse to being my wife in every way?"

Sable's body flamed with heat. "In other words, am I willing to sleep with you regularly?"

Huffing in aggravation, Kahner marveled at the woman's frank candor. He'd never quite known anyone who could make him this crazy.

"Yes, Sable. That is what I am asking."

"But you're not asking me to marry you. You're just asking if I'll sleep with you if I decide to marry you rather than be relocated elsewhere."

"Oh, good grief!"

"Put yourself in my shoes, Kahner! The last few days have been a whirlwind of change, and name changes for that matter. I just found out yesterday who you are, and I'm not sure yet that knowing your real name means I know who you truly are! I get the feeling you're not telling me something. Clearly, there is something different about this household; your family."

Kahner stood, peering down upon Sable with a calculating stare. She was obviously referencing his brother Kalabernus.

Becoming uneasy at his fierce gaze Sable refused to let the man get under her skin. "Look, I get it okay. Considering the precarious position that I'm in, I get that marrying you will help hide me and my children and keep us safe. There are just so many unanswered questions here, and it feels like I'm being asked to make a decision based on limited information."

"What do you need to know?"

"Would this be permanent or...?"

"Yes," Kahner responded, interrupting her.

"I see," Sable spoke slowly, deliberately as she swallowed hard. "And your intent is to adopt my children, but does that mean you'll actually be a father to them? Or is that pretend too?"

"I have every intention of raising them as though they were my own," Kahner replied with a scowl. She was making it sound like everything was simply a ploy to throw off Lionel and Kobi Radford.

"And where will we live?"

"Here."

Startled, Sable gazed around the living room. "You mean, here with your father and brother?"

"The house one day falls to me as I am the eldest, but yes. Dad tends to stay in his own part of the house or works the stables, so you likely won't be bothered by him much."

"And Kalabernus?"

"I'm afraid his presence here is a permanent situation."

"Kalturek said yesterday that Kalabernus was likely never going to be able to leave this house. Why? Is it because he's touched in the head?"

"He's not touched in the head!" Kahner said sharply, taking exception to her use of words.

Seeing she'd made him cross Sable raised her hand in a gesture of peace. "I'm sorry. You're right. You said he sees, what was it, shadows or demons is it?"

Kahner exhaled. "Yes."

He appeared troubled.

"I'm just trying to understand, Kahner. It's a little confusing. These shadows, or demons as you call them; are you referring to fallen angels? And has he always seen them? Should I be worried he might hurt my kids?" she asked urgently. "Do these shadows tell him to do things he shouldn't or something?"

"Fallen angels? I suppose if you believe that sort of thing, yes. I would imagine some might refer to them like that." Kahner could see Sable nodding with understanding.

"When I was a child I attended both my father's church as well as learned the ways of my mother's people. Mom eventually converted and they would both go on these mission trips to places like Haiti and Brazil. She told me a story once about a man they came across in Brazil with a similar problem. My understanding is that it's extremely rare for one to see fallen angels."

"Shadows, Sable. Kalabernus calls them shadows or demons, and for a reason, I'd wager. You need to understand this is not a household of individuals who believe in such things as faith. My brother has been cursed with the ability to be able to see shadowy figures for as long as I can remember. He can hear them too. They talk to him. Dad tries to get him not to respond, but sometimes the troublesome three provoke him."

"The troublesome three?" Sable asked, confused by the term, wondering how a family could believe in demons but not fallen angels or angels.

"There are three figures who seem to have latched onto him and tormented him over the years. Kalabernus calls them the troublesome three. But their names are…"

"They have names?" Sable asked, alarmed by this news.

"Veranke, Fallen, and Zalman. I mention them, so you are aware of what's going on when he speaks of them. If ever you find him talking to them, you need to remove yourself and your children from his presence and come to get me."

Sable sat for a moment, thinking back to earlier in the morning when she had come out of the bathroom. Recalling what Kalabernus had been mumbling at the time she finally understood. Her gut clenched.

"They were in my room," she whispered softly, wondering at why the shadows would have been present if they were, in fact, real.

"Did you say they were in your room?" Kahner asked in surprise.

"This morning. I came out of the bathroom and Kalabernus was sitting on the bed. He was peering up at the ceiling insisting that Veranke and Zalman needed to leave me alone." Sable noted Kahner's concerned expression. "It feels like he has been following me around all day, and he says the oddest of things."

"I know he's a little unsettling at times. And if he could live on his own, he'd be able to stay at the cabin Dad built for him. But the problem here is he has nightmares because of them. So, he doesn't sleep well and will often go for days without rest."

"Such loss of sleep I would imagine would make him delirious."

"Yes, and that's exactly what happened a few years back," Kahner explained. "Apparently, in his delirium, he wandered from the cabin and got lost in the woods. He came upon campers during the night and scared them all nearly to death when he stumbled into their camp." Kahner paused in discomfort then proceeded to explain. "There were children present. Well, you can imagine a giant of a man stumbling deliriously about in the middle of the night, raving about shadows and demons… The parents caused quite a fuss over the incident and Dad decided my brother could no longer be allowed to live alone."

"I see."

"He's not dangerous, Sable. He would never physically hurt your children. He loves kids. Truly he is a giant among men with a heart of a teddy bear. But I won't lie to you. Kalabernus might unintentionally frighten them without meaning to."

Taking it all in, Sable stared into the fireplace, watching the embers burning brightly within. The snap and crack of the fire soothed her already jangled nerves. Brow furrowing in thought, she couldn't help but feel pity for Kahner's brother. When she'd first met him, she'd sensed a 'darkness' about him but he'd also seemed very gentle and even kind. Yet she couldn't get past the uneasy sensation she experienced when near him. Now she understood why. Shadowy figures had latched onto him. Whether demonic or not, Sable somehow now realized that was the presence she was feeling near him, seemingly always ever present.

Chapter 15

Two days later the entire family gathered for dinner to meet Kahner's fiancée and her children. Arriving first, Synedra's husband, Nathan Kayme, began hauling trays of food into the kitchen from the back end of his sports utility vehicle.

"Where's Synedra?" Kahner called out to Nathan who disappeared through the kitchen doors. Returning moments later, Nathan crossed his arms over his chest and frowned at his brother-in-law.

"You gonna help me haul this in, or just keep sitting there staring at the newspaper you're pretending to read?"

Kahner scowled back at Nathan. "You didn't answer my question. Where's your wife?"

"Your sister will be along shortly. She had a last-minute customer at the shop," Nathan responded. "Now get out here and help me. Bastion insisted I pick up dinner from The Boar's Head rather than attempting, as he put it, 'to muddle around with a mess himself.' Apparently, he doesn't put much faith in yours or your fiancée's cooking?"

"One burnt meal and he has marked us both as incompetents in the kitchen," Kahner grumbled. He folded his newspaper and stood. "I told him we could just order pizza from Laynie's Pizza Emporium."

"Yes, heaven forbid we should stand on ceremony and have a real meal for a rehearsal dinner rather than pizza," Bastion vented as he strode into the living room from the hallway. "Have you seen Kalabernus?"

"No, why?" Kahner's head jerked to attention.

Bastion shook his head as though distracted. "No reason. Think I'll go check on Sable though."

Nathan watched his father-in-law disappear up the stairs. "What's that all about?"

"Kalabernus has taken to following Sable around for some reason," Kahner replied evenly, his mouth thinning with displeasure.

"I see. Should we be worried?"

"Don't know yet. Come on then. Let's get everything inside. I suspect everyone will be arriving soon. We should get the food in the oven to keep it warm."

The two men headed outside, and each grabbed a couple trays and two large brown paper bags from within the vehicle. As they were attempting to close the back end of the SUV, Kalturek and Stephanie drove up with Drayke and Laynie pulling in not far behind.

"I'll get it for you," Drayke called, stepping out of his vehicle. Shutting the door for them he took a tray and bag from Nathan.

"Yeah, okay. I see how it is," Kahner grumbled, still hampered down by two bags and trays.

"Oh, quit your griping." Kalturek grinned, strolling away from his brother toward the house, not bothering to help. "It's good for you."

Swatting her husband's arm, Stephanie laughed. "You're horrible sometimes. Here Kahner, let me help you," she said sweetly, taking a bag from his hand.

"See now, I knew there was a reason I always liked you," Kahner said with a smile reminiscent of her husband's.

"Stephanie, you're supposed to be on my side," Kalturek exclaimed in mock indignation.

"His side, your side…" Stephanie responded with an impish grin. "You both look the same, so in the end what does it really matter? Although, Kahner, dare I say it? You appear to be looking a few years older than your *identical* twin brother. I wonder why that could be?" she teased.

Stretching up onto her tiptoes Stephanie gave her brother-in-law a peck on the cheek. "It's good to see you home, Kahner. Is it for good this time?" she asked softly.

Kahner noted his sister-in-law seemed shorter than usual. Realizing it was because she wasn't wearing her typical high heels, he nodded in the affirmative. Kahner moved towards the path to the patio.

"Yup, I brought me home a fiancée and kids too."

"I heard," Stephanie's face fell instantly. Pulling herself back together she smiled bravely then followed Drayke and Laynie along the path.

Reaching the patio decking, Laynie turned at the sound of another vehicle pulling up the long drive.

"Looks like Mackenzie and her husband S.T. have arrived," Laynie said, shielding her eyes from the early evening sun. She could see the black Lexus pull up behind their vehicle, and a long black-haired petite figure hopped out.

"Yeah, but no Synedra yet," Kahner responded, pausing in the doorway as he glanced back. He frowned in frustration.

"What? Our glorious presence isn't enough for you?" Drayke inquired, feigning a wounded expression, yet all the while appearing suspicious.

"Oh, shut it," Kahner replied good-naturedly, attempting to mask his disappointment at his sister's absence. He was anxious for Synedra to meet Sable but didn't want to tip anyone off as to why. Catching his brother Kalturek's eye he shifted his gaze toward Stephanie guiltily, then away quickly.

Everyone moved into the kitchen and began setting up for the dinner. Pulling plates, cups, and silverware from the cupboards they set the dining room tables and began prepping the trays of food on the long counter. The camaraderie among his siblings and their spouses bolstered his spirits. Kahner found he could relax for the first time in days.

"Where is the fiancée anyway?" Laynie asked curiously after a bit. She peered around the kitchen, craning her slender neck for anyone new that might be the woman in question.

"Yeah, where's the fiancée Kahner?" Mackenzie mimicked. She stepped into the kitchen with her husband, Dr. S.T. Funnie following at her heels. "Are you hiding her somewhere?" she asked, then stopped short at the sight of him. "Or more accurately, what is it you're hiding from us, Kahner?"

Everyone stopped abruptly at what they were doing and stared in Kahner's direction.

"Haven't a clue what you're talking about," Kahner replied in denial.

Sensing a presence coming up behind him, Kahner turned to see Sable entering the kitchen from the hallway with his father and her three kids in tow. Bastion looked troubled and Sable was fidgeting anxiously as though she'd been spooked.

"Everything okay?" Kahner inquired, unable to mask the worry in his tone. He noted Sable's hands were shaking. Glancing toward his father, one eyebrow rose in question.

"Kalabernus will be along shortly. He's currently cleaning paint off her bedroom wall," Bastion said in reply.

"Paint?" Drayke asked, shooting a look towards his brother Kalturek.

Lisa giggled nervously and gazed up at her mother looking slightly confused. "He must really like to paint too," she said only to be interrupted by her brother Jordan.

"Yeah, Kalabernus made red crosses all over mama's bedroom wall," Jordan said as Adam shook his head in affirmation, his eyes wide as though in dismay.

"Red crosses," Mackenzie exclaimed. "Wait a minute, which room did you put her in?" she asked her father anxiously.

"Your old room," Bastion said evenly.

Mackenzie stamped her feet. "Dad! Why did you…?"

"What's all the commotion?" A soft lilting voice came from the hallway as Synedra strolled into the kitchen with a large flowered bag in hand. She was peering down into the bag as she walked and appeared to be searching for something. "Ah, got it. Here, Stephanie. I believe this was what you were asking for, right?" Synedra inquired, handing off a small jar to her sister-in-law.

"Oh, yes, thank you! My skin has been so dry lately." Stephanie responded gratefully. It was rather nice having a sister-in-law who owned an Herbal shop that sold homemade lotions and remedies. Her stuff always seemed to work so much better than the store-bought brands.

"This is the fiancée, eh?" Synedra asked, hiking the bag over her shoulder. She eyed the woman briefly with the same shimmering blue eyes that the rest of her siblings had. Her medium-length, straight black hair hung loosely about her face.

Sable could feel all their bright pale blue eyes upon her. It was more than a little bit disconcerting after the discovery of the red crosses all over her bedroom walls. Licking her lips self-consciously, she pushed her hair out of the way of her eyes.

"Yes, so it would seem. I'm Sable. Sable Kryder," she stammered, cringing when she realized she'd almost given the wrong name again. Her head was spinning a bit. Feeling a hand on her elbow she realized Bastion was attempting to steady her as she extended her hand in greeting.

Shaking hands with the woman, Synedra smiled and walked past Kahner, her gaze never wavering from his. Dumping her bag on a chair she headed toward the pantry.

"I see dinner's ready. The Boar's Head, eh?" Synedra commented, noting the logo on the brown bags. "Go ahead without me. I'll join everyone in a minute," Synedra called, disappearing into the pantry.

Grabbing plates from the tables, Dr. S.T. handed one to his wife Mackenzie, then headed straight for the counter laden with food.

"Don't mind if I do. I'm famished," Dr. S.T. said hungrily, eyeing the roast beef and mashed potatoes with appreciation.

The clamor and clatter of plates and chairs scooting in and out resounded through the kitchen as everyone filled their plates and took their seats. Assisting Sable with plates for the kids, Kahner helped settle them at a table, and then grabbed one of his own.

Wandering back into the kitchen, Synedra prepared a tea kettle with water and set it to heat. Humming while she worked, as the rest of the family dug into their meal, she pulled down a mug from the cupboard and placed a tea bag within. While waiting for the water to boil, she filled a plate of her own and set it at the empty seat next to her husband, Nathan. Returning to the stove upon hearing the tea kettle whistling, she poured the hot water into the mug and carried it toward the table.

Chatting amiably with the family members as they pestered Kahner and probed her with questions, Sable almost missed seeing Synedra switch out her coffee mug for another. Eyeing the woman curiously Sable realized her stomach was becoming unsettled and that she was thirsty.

"I think you'll find that will help," Synedra thought, being careful not to speak aloud.

"Sorry, help with what?" Sable inquired, reaching for the mug Synedra had set before her. Blinking, Sable suddenly realized the woman's mouth had never moved. "Wait, did you just say something to me?"

Synedra turned toward Kahner who was staring avidly at the two women with a calculating look.

"Shame on you, Kahner," Synedra thought playfully, knowing her brother would hear her. "You do realize Laynie, and especially Stephanie, are going to be pissed when they find out?"

"Find out what? Why are Laynie and Stephanie going to be mad?" Sable asked, having drawn everyone's attention. She was responding to questions the rest of the family couldn't hear.

"Synedra, why did you switch Sable's mug?" Bastion inquired, his voice sharp, his eyes alert. His gaze shifted between the two women.

Startled, Sable stared at the woman in surprise then down at her mug. What was going on?

The silence that followed was unsettling, almost eerie, as Synedra took her seat at the table completely unfazed by everyone's inquiring eyes.

"What did you just give her?" Mackenzie asked, sensing Kahner's excitement as well as instant anger among others.

"Is that what I think it is?" Stephanie inquired, gesturing toward the mug in Sable's hand. Her anger and resentment were almost palpable.

"Synedra!" Mackenzie called sharply across the table, gaining her sister's attention. "Did you just give her Lemon Balm Tea?"

Taking up her fork, Synedra shifted in her seat then nonchalantly forked a bite of roast beef. "But of course. Sable is pregnant with Kahner's baby after all. She's gonna need it."

"Don't you mean babies?" Kalabernus said unexpectedly from the hallway.

Sable had barely the time to recover from the shock of Synedra's statement before Kalabernus had appeared. Gaping openly at him as he stood in the entryway to the kitchen, peering around the room, she noted his eyes were wild and sweat was beading along his brow.

"Did you say, babies – plural?" Laynie exclaimed. Slamming her silverware on the table she stood suddenly and glared across the table at Drayke, then Sable.

"Yup. Troublesome three seem awful agitated by it for some reason too," Kalabernus replied, seemingly distracted as he scratched at his forehead. His haunted pale blue eyes shifted around the room, appearing to almost glow against his tanned skin.

"Wait a minute. Is that why you painted red crosses on my old bedroom wall?" Mackenzie inquired in astonishment. "Because of those loathsome blasted shadows?"

"More importantly," Stephanie piped in. Wiping her mouth with a napkin she tossed it on the table and got up from her seat as well. Turning toward Kalabernus she placed her hands on her narrow hips and stared him down. "Are the troublesome three saying she's having more than one baby?" she asked irately. She pointed toward Sable who still sat holding the mug in her hand looking shocked.

"Like father like son, she will have more than one," Kalabernus declared. "Of course, that's what the shadows are saying, and we all know how honest they can be. But I tend to believe them this time."

"Why?" Bastion wanted to know.

Kalabernus blinked then looked back at his father. Rubbing his red paint splattered hands together he shrugged, and then fixed Sable with a penetrating stare.

"Because they don't like her," Kalabernus explained, his tone becoming serious. "Veranke wants to maim her and kill the babies. You shouldn't have made me clean the paint off the walls, Dad. They didn't like the crosses either for some reason."

Chapter 16

"Sable, wait!" Kahner hollered.

Erupting from his chair he dashed across the room after Sable's fleeing form, ignoring the angry shouts of his brother's wives and the ensuing fight among them.

Disappearing into the living room, Sable paced back and forth in front of the fireplace. Her hands were clasped about her head and she was murmuring frantically.

"Sable, we need to talk…"

"Talk about what Kahner?" Sable shouted, her anger getting the better of her. "What the hell is going on here?"

"Listen to me…"

"No! No, you listen. I want answers and none of this bullshit about telling me family secrets later!" she yelled, not caring that his family could likely hear her from the kitchen. "Why does your sister Synedra think I am pregnant, and why does Kalabernus think I'm having multiple babies?"

"Actually, he said like father like son, which I believe technically means he thinks you're expecting triplets." Kahner wished instantly from the florid and horrified expression on her face that he hadn't said that.

"Triplets?" Sable gaped at him. "You can't be serious with this."

"Try and calm down," Kahner thought. "Please, Sable." Intentionally not speaking as he stared directly at her, Kahner watched the play of emotions cross her face. He could tell she'd heard him.

"You want me to calm down?" Sable asked, knowing even as she said it that he hadn't said anything. But how could that be? Grabbing at her head she spun in place. What was wrong with her? Was she going crazy?

"You're not going crazy," Kahner said aloud. Taking her by the shoulders, he turned her toward him, forcing her to look him in the eye. "But you do know what I'm thinking now, don't you?" he thought while staring her down.

Sable stared back at him frantically. "How is this possible?" she asked, beginning to panic as she trembled. "How is it that I… that I can…?"

"Say it, Sable, say it aloud," Kahner urged her with his mind, not speaking a word.

"I can read your thoughts?" Sable exclaimed, her voice rising as though in question.

Kahner nodded urgently. "Yes, Sable. You can hear my thoughts, and I suspect others as well. It's why you've been having so much trouble with Kalabernus the last few days."

Eyes wide in dismay, Sable shook with the shock of the truth in his words. "But how? How can I read people's thoughts?" she asked desperately, all the while thinking she had to have lost her mind. The instant she spoke the question, Sable somehow just knew she already had the answer.

"It's true, isn't it?" Sable asked, her eyes flashing. "I'm pregnant. Is that it? Is that the key here? Because I'm pregnant with your child I'm able to read people's thoughts?"

Kahner inhaled sharply. He sensed more than saw when Mackenzie was standing in the doorway to the living room. "Not now, Mackenzie," he ground out.

"You have to tell her Kahner. She's frightened and becoming angry with you." Mackenzie insisted, worried at the woman's reaction. She hoped desperately that Sable wouldn't turn into another Eliza.

"How does she know that?" Sable asked Kahner. "How do you know that?" she inquired of Mackenzie resentfully. "And who's Eliza?"

"Mackenzie, like the rest of my children, is gifted with certain powers," Bastion said matter-of-factly. Having come into the living room he stood before the couple, his blue eyes shimmering between the two of them. "And as for Eliza… I'd say it's time Kahner. You must tell her everything or history will repeat itself." Giving his son a fierce look, Bastion turned on his heel and disappeared down the hall, no longer interested in the meal. He could hear his other two sons arguing with their wives in the kitchen and suspected there would be plenty of leftovers for the next few days.

"What does he mean by that?" Sable asked, turning her narrowed gaze upon Kahner. "What is he talking about, history repeating itself?"

"I will explain everything, but it's going to take a little time," Kahner replied, watching as she shoved her hand roughly against her belly. "Let's get you that tea Synedra made for you. Then we'll sit and talk. I'll tell you everything you need to know and some you won't want to know."

"Why? And what's that tea supposed to do? Why did she give it to me?" Sable asked suspiciously, worried at what it might be that he needed to tell her that she wouldn't want to know.

"My sister Synedra is gifted with the ability to heal, or more accurately, know what is ailing a person. It's why she markets her own herbal teas and home remedies as well as lotions and what-not. Her store butts up against her husband Nathan's detective agency. That's how they met. It's also how she knew instantly that you were pregnant," Kahner explained while accepting the mug of tea from Synedra, who had just carried it into the room for Sable. "This is Lemon Balm Tea. It helps aid with calming nausea in women who are…"

"Pregnant," Sable finished for him. Taking the proffered mug, she eyed it carefully then glanced toward Synedra who was now standing next to her sister in the doorway. "So, she's just trying to help me?"

"Yes, it's what I do," Synedra answered for her brother and then disappeared into the kitchen.

"And Mackenzie?"

"She senses people's emotions."

"Right. Of course, she does," Sable said with a nervous laugh. "What about the rest of you? Bastion said you're all gifted?" Her stomach churned uneasily causing her to lift the cup to her lips. Taking a tentative sip, she noted it had a light lemony scent.

"Or cursed," Kahner replied grimly. "Depends on your point of view."

"You mean because Kalabernus can see the shadows?"

Nodding, Kahner helped Sable take a seat on the couch. Joining her there, he propped one knee up on the couch and turned toward her.

"Now Kalturek, he can see auras around people."

"You mean, like different colors of light surrounding them, depending on their mood?" Sable asked, having heard of such things in movies and stories.

"Sort of. He either sees a black shadowy haze or a bright, almost white, light. Usually, it only encompasses around one's head from shoulder to shoulder. We think it's more like good versus evil intentions that he's seeing," Kahner explained while gesturing with his hand over his head from one side of his body to the next. "For example, a teenager going into a drugstore might have a black aura but as he comes out it might be white, having decided not to rob the store."

"Okay," Sable said slowly, attempting to take it all in. She could see Kahner was visibly nervous for some reason and he rarely, if ever, lost his composure, which made her anxious. "And your brother, Drayke?"

Chuckling Kahner gave a half smile as he fidgeted, knowing full well how crazy he must sound. "Ah, well, Drayke's is the ability we all envy and wish we had."

"Why?"

"Because he can decipher when someone is lying."

"Wait, what?"

"Kind of like when you told everyone your name was Sable Kryder," Drayke piped in from the kitchen. Bobbing his head around the door frame, Drayke stared intently out at his brother. "Now why do you suppose that is? Who is she really, Kahner?"

"Drop it, Drayke," Bastion said forcefully from the hallway, having returned from his foray to the study. In his hand, he was carrying a large leather-bound book.

Eyeing his father intently, Drayke shrugged. "Fine. It's dropped," he said simply. Glancing back at Sable curiously, he disappeared back into the kitchen.

"I'll watch your kids," Bastion said, striding toward them with a book in hand. Passing it off to his son, he continued, "Best start at the beginning, Kahner."

Taking a deep breath Kahner exhaled, peering down at the book in his hands. Fingering the cover anxiously, his gaze shifted toward Sable, wondering if he could trust her or not.

"You're worried about whether you can trust me when I'm the one supposedly pregnant by a man with powers who failed to tell me about it?" Sable queried with disgust. She appeared visibly wounded by his thoughts which gave Kahner pause.

"I'm about to share with you something that no one outside this family is aware of," he said in his defense.

"There's more than you all having certain powers?" Sable asked. "I take it that isn't well known by many either?"

"You would be correct."

Sipping her tea, Sable peered down at her cup, realizing she'd already somehow managed to drink nearly half of it and didn't remember doing so. Setting the cup down she let out a whoosh of air then turned to face Kahner with an intent gaze.

"Is it safe to assume that these `gifts,' or `powers' as you call them, are inherited?"

"Yes," Kahner replied. "My father tends to know things without knowing why, and he can often see future events."

With a loud derisive laugh, Sable groaned. "Right, and I bet Bastion saw me coming," she said as her laughter filtered off into a nervous chuckle. She was still struggling to believe everything she was hearing.

Tilting his head toward her thoughtfully Kahner replied, "In a way, I think he did."

"Really? How so?" she asked, giving him a disbelieving look.

"I have had that packet of identities for nearly fifteen years," Kahner muttered. Leaning toward her, he whispered in a low tone. "Where do you think I got the name Sable Kryder in the first place?"

Chapter 17

Yes, Bastion had indeed seen Sable coming.

What the RavenCroft children didn't know was that he had a vision within a few days of Kahner's announcement about applying to the CIA. Bastion didn't know the exact details of the situation, nor had he known exactly who she was until she had told him, or when it all would transpire, but something within the vision had prompted him to prepare multiple forms of identification for a woman, three children, and his son. So, when Kahner took the job within the CIA, he took the packet of identities with him and was told to always have it close by.

Smart thinking on Bastion's part, wouldn't you say?

It seems either the Fates, God, or whoever oversaw the universe had been watching out for them this time. What Bastion had not foreseen, or anticipated, was the discovery that Sable would be the former wife of a drug lord who had proof a high-ranking official within the CIA was having dealings with the same men she was running from. Nor had he known Kahner's reasons for returning home would be because of the risk of discovery by his own estranged brother of nearly fifty-seven years. Obviously, this complicated matter.

Bastion also had not known she'd wind up pregnant with triplets by his son. This, at least, came as a delightful shock to him. But he was worried and with good reason. Sable already had a lot to deal with on her own. The bruising still prevalent upon her face, and her cautious, untrusting manner, led Bastion to believe she'd been dealt some unkind blows in many ways. To add being pregnant with gifted children to the mix might well be too much for her. Then there was the added worry, that if she refused to have Kahner's children and marry his son, would they be able to trust her with their secret if she were relocated with her children elsewhere?

- - -

"On a more positive note, if you stay here in the RavenCroft valley and marry me you'll never ever have to worry about Lionel finding you and the kids."

"Why does everyone keep speaking of where we're at as if it is its own entity. The RavenCroft valley. Shouldn't it be more like the RavenCroft horse ranch? Seems to me that would make more sense. It's not like you can possibly own the whole valley."

Kahner chuckled. "In a way we kind of do. It was our ancestors, the Croft's who founded this location initially. The Raven portion of our name was added much later." He paused in thought. "Do you remember when Kalturek drove us here? When we reached the property line the kids became excited over the swarms of ravens they saw?"

"Yes, it was like watching a murmuration of starlings. They were twisting and turning as if they were all connected as they flew across the sky, changing direction and course at a moment's notice. Then they settled together in a blanket of black feathers across the grounds." Sable recalled being alarmed at the sight of so many ravens all in one place. She'd always been taught by her grandmother that seeing one was a bad omen. What did it mean, if there were hundred's?

"This valley we're located in along with the immediate surrounding area has always been inhabited by ravens. It's their sanctuary. But we don't bother them, so they don't bother us. And they're just one of the reasons why Lionel and Kobi won't ever find you here. But it's mostly because of the surrounding environment."

"How do you figure that?" she wondered.

"How many people do you know who would willing walk into a valley filled with black ravens?"

"Fair point." Still, she couldn't help but think he didn't fully grasp her situation. Lionel and Kobi had people all over the world. She wondered silently how he could be so sure they wouldn't find them in the RavenCroft valley.

Knowing full well what she was thinking, Kahner took a deep breath, launching into the explanation his father gave him and his brothers when they turned twelve years old and came fully into their abilities. "This isn't just a sanctuary for the ravens, though they were here long before our Croft ancestors took possession of this land. There are apparently pockets of acreage around the world, protected by an unseen force. Or at least, we're aware of a total of three locations so far. For all we know, there could be more. Where you are right now – RavenCroft valley – is but one of those."

"What do you mean by protected? And how is it you can be so sure no one else knows of this valley and these other two locations you speak of?" What he was saying sounded absurd.

"Because this land we're located on, just like the other two, cannot be seen by anyone outside our family unless we allow them to. If someone gets close to the bordering edge of the valley they become disoriented and eventually either turn around or go around. In order to find a way in, three things have to happen; you have to be gifted in some way, you must be told by someone in our bloodline of its location, and you must also be bound to the individual in marriage. It's why we never invite guests over or host parties. No one outside of our family has ever been in the valley and that must stay that way."

Sable snorted. What he was telling her sounded ridiculous, like a joke. Taking in his pensive expression she realized he wasn't kidding. "Your being serious right now. You actually believe this."

"Yes, and it's not just that I believe it. It's a documented fact, recorded in journals by the Croft family ever since they moved here. The fact that I am telling you this now, before we're married, is significant because knowing this can be dangerous. Not just for you but for the rest of my family as well. I'm only telling you this now because after what you've been through, you deserve to know what you're getting into, and we feel you need to know the true advantage you'd have here if you stay. But if you choose to be relocated elsewhere, you'd be taking our secret with you, out there, where anyone could get to you, and by extension, us. So I'm taking a huge risk telling you this. You need to understand how serious this really is, Sable, because people have actually died to protect the valley and this family."

Her belly started doing flip flops. Why did it feel like she was standing on the edge of a precipice, waiting to fall over?

"I'd promise not to say anything," she said in a small voice, laughing nervously at the dark look he cast her way. "Even if I did, I doubt anyone would believe me anyways. It sounds like something one would read in a fantasy novel."

He winced, not liking the direction she'd just gone. "There are some who would take you very seriously. You have to understand, this secret has been tightly kept for over two hundred years by every descendent of the Croft family who first discovered this valley and settled here back in the early 1800's. They were like us, gifted with extraordinary abilities, even though my father does not actually extend from the original Croft family."

Sable frowned, confused by his last statement. Bastion RavenCroft wasn't of that lineage? And when had the family name gone from Croft to RavenCroft?

"Long story short, my ancestor, Leapold Croft renamed himself Croft after an accidental extended period of time staying within the valley without venturing out. There's a whole journal on that particular incident, in order to help aid the rest of us from avoiding the same issue."

Okay, that was getting annoying. "Would you stop doing that? Stop reading my mind, it's so disconcerting."

Kahner cringed. "Sorry. Sometimes I can't help it, particularly when its right there on the surface. You'll understand soon. And I know that's confusing but I'll explain what I mean by the time thing in a minute.

This valley was a Godsend to the Croft's when they discovered it because it helped protect them from some...unsavory people who were avidly searching for them. It also kept them safe from the many greedy panhandlers that flooded the area during the Pikes Peak gold rush of 1859." There was more to that part of the story but he figured it best to hold some of the details back until he knew for sure what her decision was. He knew his father would not want him sharing that information yet.

"I'm confused, you said we were in Loveland." Recalling the Colorado map she'd been looking at earlier in the day with her kids, she realized what he said couldn't be true. "Pike's Peak is near Colorado Springs but Loveland is farther north of that. Why would they need protection from the panhandlers near Pike's Peak if we're in Loveland?" she asked suspiciously.

His response was sheepish. "About that. We're not actually in Loveland right now." Sable huffed angrily, spurring him quickly to his defense. "Technically, I didn't lie to you though. And the gold diggers were all over these mountains at one point. Pike's Peak was simply the most well-known of the stories of gold being found at the time."

"And technically I'm supposed to be dead, and therefore, no longer married to Lionel, which is the only way a marriage between us would even be possible right now. But we both know that's not technically true either," she snapped.

"You asked where we were and I responded that the address for our home is listed as Loveland, Colorado."

"That's a very fine line your walking there," she warned. "And why does the valley, and have a Loveland address if it's located in, what? Colorado Springs?"

"No, we're much further north, but still south of Drake, Colorado. We're located in a hidden valley on the western outskirts of Loveland near Larimer County. Dad has all our mail sent to an address in Loveland, in order to help keep our location a secret. He usually has Kalturek pick it up on his way home from work at the Loveland Sheriff's department.

Or sometimes Laynie or my brother Drayke will pick it up when he can't since they work out of Loveland too."

"There's a Drake, Colorado and your brother's name is Drayke?" Kahner chuckled and nodded in response. She was starting to have trouble keeping everything straight.

The grandfather clock chimed, startling Sable out of her thoughtful reverie. Sitting poised before the fire, her head down, she contemplated what he told her so far. She felt like she was a character in one of those supernatural flicks where the heroine suddenly discovered a world of vampires and werewolves were real. Only in this case the RavenCroft's were human's with special powers, not shapeshifters or immortals. Turning her head she gazed at him thoughtfully, his beautiful eyes transfixing her. He really was exceptionally good looking. She was having difficulty gauging his age. And his father looked to be fifty rather than sixty. It made her wonder how old he was.

Smiling broadly, Kahner's eyes twinkled as he chuckled again, having read her mind. "No, we're not immortal. We can become ill and die just like everyone else. That said..."

"Oh, here we go..." Sable erupted from her chair, hands fluttering as she started to pace. She didn't bother nailing him for the whole mind reading thing again. What was the point?

"Now wait a minute. Stop. Sable calm down. All I was going to tell you is that our aging process does tend to be slowed by the fact we live where we do. If you stay...it would have the same effect on you."

"How? Why? And how old exactly are you?" She was flustered, her mind racing. If she married him and lived in the valley she wouldn't age as fast? That was every woman's dream – to look younger than they were. Now she knew she had to be asleep. She pinched herself. The sharp pain causing her to yelp. Her pacing became frantic after that and she kept banging her legs up against the ottoman every time she passed it. At one point she faltered and had to catch herself by pushing off from the ottoman in order to keep from falling.

"Time seems to run more slowly here than it does outside of the valley. What could be a month out there amounts to about a week in here."

"That would explain a lot." Seeing the look he threw her way she went on. "When we first arrived it was a Monday. Four days later your brother said it was Tuesday. He was very adamant about it and we argued. He got real upset, then confused, and suddenly blustered that he had to go check his, and I quote, special calendar. What he said didn't make sense at the time but now..."

"The calendars, yes. We all have specialized calendars we keep to track our days. Dad recently converted them to digital form so we can keep them on our laptops or Ipads. We're able to do this because Dad's father invented a special clock that has four hands on it. He made it over forty years ago. He recognized the importance of needing to keep better track as people started having jobs outside of the ranch, and he didn't want to make the same mistake Leopold had. It also has days, months and years on it. It's an amazing piece of work. It helps us keep track of time within time when we're out of time, for the most part. There are occasions when we still get messed up though. Particularly towards the end of the year. Deciphering the correct New Year day can be a pain."

His explanation was giving her a headache. "I don't understand. How is what you're talking about even possible?"

Daniel shrugged. "What kind of force it is that allows for these pockets of space where time seems to stand still, or rather, slow, is forever being debated amongst us. Our only written plausible explanation for this, and it's a tenuous theory at best as far as I'm concerned, is in this book. It would have us believe that the pockets of space were created by the Fates so we would have a safe place to hide from those who sought to destroy anyone believed to be involved with sorcery and witchcraft." Seeing Sable's wide-eyed expression, he hastened on. "Which we're not, of course. Magic doesn't exist."

"Says the man who can read minds."

"Says the woman who can now read minds."

At first she said nothing. Re-opening the book of lineage he had been showing her earlier in their discussion, she suddenly laughed when she caught sight of the poem he read to her. "Does it say why the maid wished for these powers?"

Kahner squirmed, not entirely inclined to go into this part of their background. Deciding learning everything now would be too much he opted for their partial history. But even that was a little embarrassing. "From what I gather, and according to this book of Lineage..."

"Wait a minute." Interrupting him, Sable leaned in closer, trying to get a better look at the second page of the book he laid on the table. It was very old and she noticed he'd put gloves on his hands. "That says it's the Blackthorne family lineage, not Croft or RavenCroft."

"Remember earlier when I mentioned dad wasn't descended from the original Crofts? He was adopted. His birth name was Randulf Blackthorne. This was left with him by his biological mother along with a note. The book details his true lineage which spans over four hundred years."

"Wow! It looks to me like it spans even further." She noted it was a very thick old leather-bound book. He'd removed it from the wooden box his father handed him before he left them in the living alone. It appeared as though it had been made to be added to, but it was starting to get too many pages for the cover bloomed fuller than the binding.

"Technically it extends much further." His tone darkened. "We choose not to lay claim to the rest."

Sensing it was likely a sore subject for some reason, she opted to drop it for the time being.

"But every Blackthorne recorded in here has been gifted in one form or another. It lists their abilities. It also has pages explaining the basis for their belief that either God or Fate created these locations for people like us."

"Other descendants of yours?"

"Probably. Essentially, we've been given a safe haven to hide when someone wants to harm us. It's been repeatedly proven that those who are not gifted cannot find the valley, and by extension, us." Tapping a page of the Blackthorne lineage with a gloved hand, he regained her attention.

"In a way, you could say, when we're here, we are being taken out of time for a while. It's a little surreal going back and forth between but we manage. The cloaking quality of the valley is the reason why all our homes have been built up over the years within the borders of the valley so we have a place to come and hide if we ever have to. It's also why dad insisted on me taking up a new identity when I applied for work at the FBI."

"I see." Sable didn't really. Or she did, sort of but it was all so confusing for her. She was having difficulty wrapping her head around what she was learning. They all appeared to have their own lives outside of the valley, but when they weren't working they hid themselves away. Especially Kalabernus. The question was why? She understood they were gifted but didn't get completely what they were afraid of and who they were hiding from. People were no longer being burned at the stake or hung simply because they were different.

"I've only ever told one other this. That's how closely we guard this secret. It's so very important that we're sure of the person's trust before we say anything which is why we normally don't share our secrets about our abilities, the valley and our true background with anyone but our spouse."

Sable looked away in wonder, trying to imagine finding all this out after having married someone. "What do you people do, tell your new wife or husband on your wedding night? Is that how ST found out?"

"Yes, though I suspect he was starting to figure out something was different. They'd been dating for a while and he's pretty sharp."

"And is that before or after you sleep with them?" She asked, disgusted by the notion. She was sure that conversation often did not end well. "Seems an awful cruel thing to do, particularly to a woman. What if she gets pregnant, like in my case? Keeping something so important – a part of you – secret like that until after the fact."

Kahner rubbed his hand across his jaw. He knew firsthand how damaging that could be. His first marriage ended, in part, because of it. Shifting in his chair he leaned forward. "Because you are pregnant with my child you now have the ability to read minds. What do you think your best friend would do if they knew what you were capable of?"

Sable gave a dry laugh. "My best friend isn't even a good one on the best of days. We're more acquaintances then anything. She's always broke and in debt to someone, including my husband. She'd sell me out for an ounce of drugs. Knowing her as well as I do, I'd say she'd try and use me to rob a bank or something."

"And what if Lionel knew?"

"Are you kidding me? If he knew I was alive he'd first beat me nearly to death then only keep me alive so he could use me to ferret out everyone's secrets in his drug cartel and..." She paused her eyes going wide with understanding, for the first time taking into real consideration how dangerous such an ability could be if someone knew. There were so many ways it could be exploited both intentionally and otherwise.

By the look on her face, Kahner could see she was starting to comprehend. "Looks like you've made my point for me. We usually leave the valley only for supplies and to work, not that any of us would probably need to. It's more purely out of the desire to pursue other interests because not all of us are interested in taking over dad's horse ranch like what I am. It took a lot to get dad to agree to this arrangement too. But any other time we've agreed to hide ourselves away here," he said, indicating the house they now sat in. "With the exception of my time at the FBI, that is. It's the only place we can truly be ourselves among others like us. It's why our family is so close compared to most families these days."

It wasn't lost on Sable that he'd deemed their work pursuits were purely for enjoyment rather than the need for money. Which led her to wonder... How did they afford anything if they didn't really need to work?

Intentionally not answering her unsaid question, Kahner carefully leafed through the pages of the Blackthorne lineage to the back of the book. He pointed at a name, encouraging her to read it aloud.

"Rathbourne and Sapphire Blackthorne. Who are they?"

"*They*, are my dad's real parents. Do you need a break or are you ready for more?"

"More what? You mean secrets? Geez Kahner, how many more are there?"

"Honey, we're descendants from a family of people who may very well be able to lay claim to a lineage that extends back to the fairy people of old. We're bound to have a *ton* of secrets."

Chapter 18

The clock chimed near the entryway signifying the late hour. It was an old grandfather's clock which stood over five feet in height. The maple wood finish had been meticulously tended to over the years, for it barely showed its age.

Resting her head on the couch, Sable stared down at the leather-bound book in her lap. After a bit, her gaze flitted back toward the fire. Heaving yet another long-suffering sigh, she shifted on the couch and tucked the afghan around her more snuggly.

Kahner's siblings left for their respective homes several hours before, many having skipped eating dinner. Sable's own tummy grumbled angrily for she herself had forgotten about eating until that moment. Kahner had filled her head with so much information, and he was right, some of it she wished she didn't know.

His family had a troubled past indeed. It all seemed to stem from a branch of his father's family, which Kahner's grandmother Sapphire had effectively cut off from her son, Bastion, nearly fifty-seven years before.

At the age of three, Bastion and his two brothers, Rafe and Rourke, had been playing near a stream not far from their house near Kalispell, Montana. Per Kahner's grandmother Sapphire, one of his dad's brothers had bet the other that Bastion, who at the time had been known as Randulf, couldn't cross the stream. Taking his brother up on the bet Bastion waded into the stream, laughing as he went. Turning about, expecting to see both his brothers following behind, he instead found himself pummeled into the waters, his head held under until he'd drowned. Or so Bastion's father Rathbourne Blackthorne believed.

Weeping at the sight of her son's lifeless body being carried into the house, Sapphire had insisted, in her hysterics, that she was to be left alone with him to grieve.

When Bastion's father Rathbourne left to go purchase a casket, Sapphire discovered that Bastion, then known as Randulf, was alive. Fully managing to revive him, Sapphire whisked him away to Colorado after tricking her husband Rathbourne into believing his son was still dead and that they had buried him.

In the end, Bastion had been adopted by the RavenCroft's. Bastion grew up in Loveland, Colorado on the RavenCroft horse ranch, away from the Blackthorne side of his family. According to what Kahner told Sable, his grandfather Rathbourne Blackthorne had originated from

Scotland but immigrated to Kalispell, Montana once he'd married his wife Sapphire, whom he'd loved dearly. Rathbourne, it seemed, had been a very religious man, who had been gifted with what he'd termed as `discerning abilities,' or `gifts from God.' Sapphire Blackthorne, on the other hand, having been born and raised a Romani well versed in the dark arts, did not believe in religion, and sought to squelch such beliefs in her sons to no avail. But with the incident at the river, she saw Bastion's supposed death as an opportunity to save at least one of her sons from growing up having religion imposed upon him. And not knowing which of her identical twin sons had attempted to drown Bastion, Sapphire additionally felt it was the best way to protect him from his brothers.

Sable could only imagine the hardship and subterfuge required of Sapphire in order to relocate her third child to a whole other state. Knowing she'd allowed Bastion to be adopted and raised by someone else boggled her mind, and yet she knew she'd do the same if she'd felt her child was in danger. In a way, she had or was doing just that. After all, if she agreed to Kahner's plan, she would be set to marry him on Friday and would be allowing her own three children to be raised by someone other than their own father. Not that Lionel Radford had ever been much of a father to them.

The fire crackled lightly, gaining her attention as it snapped and popped from the shifting of a log in the hearth. Re-opening the book before her, Sable leafed with a gloved hand to the page which listed the family tree. It went back so far, she thought. She'd never seen a lineage so extensive and well documented. There were nearly four hundred years of Blackthorne's alone that had been meticulously scrolled out in varying hands. But their heritage extended back even further, for they were linked to the Weir-deVere's of Scotland. From what she leafed through so far, Kahner's family was able to document over seventeen hundred years of their origins and she had only managed to get through half of the book so far. She was curious to see how far back it really went. Obviously, it had been handed down by many a generation leaving Sable to wonder how and why Kahner's grandmother Sapphire had procured the book and left it with Bastion.

Per Kahner, his grandmother Sapphire had been gifted as well. From the way he talked, Bastion received his gift of knowing things without knowing why from his father Rathbourne and his gift to foreshadow events or know the future from his mother Sapphire.

"I can only imagine what that must have been like growing up, to have such gifts," Sable murmured softly as her gloved fingertips skimmed the fragile page before her then flipped it over.

At some point, the name Randulf Blackthorne had been crossed off and replaced with Bastion RavenCroft. Sable presumed it had been penned by his own hand for it appeared to be strong, distinct penmanship; that of a man's hand. Next to his name he'd written Inara RavenCroft, which had been the name of his wife; Kahner's mother. Below that he'd written in his first three sons, the triplets: Kahner,

Kalabernus, and Kalturek. Next to them were Drayke and Mackenzie who were fraternal twins, then Synedra.

Finding it curious that Bastion hadn't placed the names of his sons' and daughters-in-law in the book yet, Sable wondered if there had been a reason for it. Had he simply not taken the time or was there another explanation, she wondered.

"From what I've seen thus far in this generation, a spouse can change. Sometimes more than once."

Startled, Sable peered back over the couch and watched as Bastion entered the living room from the kitchen. In his hand, he carried a steaming mug. She hadn't even heard him moving around in the kitchen and wondered at what he was drinking.

"A hot toddy," Bastion supplied, noting Sable's narrowed and suspicious gaze his direction. "That's right keep thinking along those lines. You're getting there," he continued. Gesturing toward her with his mug he took an appreciative sip, then walked around the couch and took a seat in the chair nearest her.

"You can know a person's thoughts like Kahner?" Sable asked, somehow already knowing the answer.

"I like to think of it as having the power of telepathy, though I'm sure my twin brother's side of the family would argue the point." Bastion took another sip of his drink then spoke again. "Where do you think Kahner gets it?" He said quietly, his expression impossible to read.

"I don't understand. Kahner only told me about…"

"-My ability to know and my ability to see future events. Yes. That would be all he would tell you, of course."

"Why?"

Shrugging, he sipped leisurely at his hot toddy once again. "What he doesn't know won't hurt him."

Gaping at the man Sable stuttered. "You mean to tell me he doesn't know you can discern a person's thoughts too?" She watched as Bastion tipped his head toward her in assent appearing almost annoyed by her description of what they were capable of. "Does the rest of your family know?"

"No. Though I suspect Nathan is beginning to figure it out. Quite perceptive that man is. He most definitely chose the right field of work; being a detective."

Face registering the initial shock at the news Sable heaved yet another sigh. "I don't understand. Why are you telling me, of all people, rather than your own children?"

Bastion didn't answer right away. Leaning back in his chair he gazed into the fire as though contemplating the bright flames burning within. After a short while, he finally answered, his voice quiet and smooth as he spoke.

"Because the men in your past have not been straight with you. From my experience, women who have been given only partial truths, or none at all, can be very dangerous to this family."

"You mean, because of Eliza. Kahner told me he'd been married before; that his wife didn't know of his gift until after they were married."

"Yes, and it proved to be his demise. She was so frightened of what she carried and the powers she was experiencing that she went out and aborted them," Bastion stated, and then added as though an afterthought. "It was odd really."

"How so?"

"She didn't believe in abortion; was even a pro-life advocate."

"Then why?"

"Why indeed?" He quirked his brow in a thoughtful gesture. Bringing his mug to his lips, he took a long drink then set the mug down.

"You believe Eliza was expecting triplets too?" She asked, having caught his plural usage.

"It would seem to be a distinct possibility. Wouldn't you agree?"

Running both hands down the pages of the book in her lap, Sable noted every male son in the Blackthorne line appeared to have sired triplets. And from every male triplet, whether fraternal or identical they too sired triplets as well.

"It would seem so." Sable shifted uneasily under his gaze. Troubled by the arguments she overheard earlier in the evening as Kahner had attempted to share his history, Sable debated on what to say next.

"Ask away. I can tell you have questions burning within you yet." Bastion's face was impassive and hard to read.

"I was just wondering… Laynie and Stephanie; they were so upset at the news."

"Yes, they would be. They've been trying for years to have children; Stephanie and Kalturek in particular."

"And Mackenzie and Synedra?"

"The same." Bastion's lips pursed grimly. He knew full well where Sable was going with her line of questioning and didn't like it.

"But Kahner…"

"Would seem to be my only hope for grandchildren – yes."

Sable stared at the book before her, a thought formulating within her mind. "Is it because he is the firstborn?"

Bastion's brows rose ever so slightly. "Interesting notion. Why do you ask?"

"Because for every family member listed here, the firstborn always seems to be the first to sire children, except for the line here."

"And which line would you be referring to?" He leaned forward to see what she was looking at.

"This one here of your brother, Rafe." She pointed toward the name on the page. "His daughters have had children so far but not his sons. Curious, isn't it?"

"Indeed," Bastion said, not wanting her to know he hadn't noticed that himself. He wondered if there was significance to it.

Sable eyed the gentleman before her then exhaled an exasperated sigh. "Bastion, I just don't understand."

"What don't you…?"

Cutting him off she flung her hands out across the book in her lap, closed the book, and shook it toward him.

"You've known all this time." She gave the man a perplexed look. "You've been aware of your brothers and your father and yet Kahner told me only once have you ever made any attempt to see them - know them. And even then, you returned home without even speaking to Rafe, who even now still lives there in Montana."

"My mother Sapphire had passed on. I knew when it happened. I saw it, but I couldn't see beyond it or why," Bastion explained. "So, yes, I went looking for answers. When I arrived, it was to discover Rourke had seduced some woman Rafe had affection for. Rourke got her pregnant then refused to marry her as he'd promised. She went to his parents for help and Rourke beat her for it. And in front of Sapphire while he was in a rage, killing his own child and nearly killing the woman."

"That's horrible."

"Yes. An interesting thing to know here is this. Rafe had come to Colorado about that same time."

"What?"

Bastion nodded. "He was looking for breeding stock. He bought it from my own father in fact. What are the odds?"

"Astronomical."

"Hhhmm. So, Rafe was away when this initially went down. He returned home to learn of what Rourke had done and found Mom in a terrible state of distress and his father, Rathbourne, attempting to cover it all up. Very embarrassing for him and his family, you see." Bastion's voice lowered in contempt as he spoke. "Rafe became enraged by Rourke's behavior and his obvious lack of conscience over the matter. They got into a huge brawl at the local tavern, and Rafe nearly killed Rourke over it. Might have succeeded if the Sheriff hadn't shot him, from what I understand."

"And your mom? Sapphire?"

"Died of a broken heart," Bastion said, his voice filling with emotion at the memory. Clearing his throat, he continued. "All this is to say there's clearly bad blood in the family. Rafe appeared to be dealing with enough troubles at the time, and Rathbourne returned to Scotland with Rourke, refusing to allow him to live anywhere near where he'd buried the woman he loved and lost."

"That's so sad," Sable offered kindly.

"Sadder yet, for apparently my so-called father Rathbourne blamed Rafe more than he did Rourke for some reason."

"But why? That makes no sense. It sounds like this Rafe was defending this woman and trying to teach Rourke a lesson. Seems to me that your mother died of a broken heart upon learning her son Rourke was capable of such heinous behavior toward a woman."

"Good question. One only Rathbourne can answer, I'm afraid." Bastion's troubled gaze shifted from the fire to Sable. "But you have another question I'd wager. One not related to this story."

Sable took a deep breath, fidgeting where she sat. "Kalabernus said the `troublesome three' want to hurt me and kill the babies I'm carrying."

"You believe you are in fact pregnant?" Bastion asked, sensing she was beginning to appreciate her situation.

"How can I not?" Sable asked wearily. "You just asked me a question, yet your lips didn't move."

Bastion gave her a wry smile, his eyes lighting up in its wake. "I did, didn't I?" He chuckled.

"Can they?"

"Can who what?"

"Don't play coy with me. Can the shadows hurt me? Can they harm these babies?"

Tapping his mug on the arm of the chair Bastion peered back at her and then stood. "From my experience, and to my knowledge, the shadows cannot kill us. But they can torment us, as they do with Kalabernus, and they can cause us harm by convincing us to make bad choices."

"Bastion," Sable started quietly, her voice barely above a whisper. "Do you think… Is it possible the shadows convinced Eliza to abort her babies?"

"My dear, anything is possible. The question you need to ask yourself is this; are you going to let them win this time around?"

"But how can I defend myself against something I cannot see?" Sable rested her hand against the bare space where once her elk teeth lay near her heart.

"The problem with Eliza was that she was afraid of us from the moment she learned of our powers. I suspect the shadows played upon that fear, convincing her that her decision was the best course for everyone. So, here's my question to you. Are you afraid? And even if you are, can you see past that fear to allow those around you to assist in protecting you?"

"You mean Kalabernus more so than Kahner, don't you?"

"Kalabernus is able to see them," Bastion acknowledged. "But I believe being bound to Kahner in marriage would give you an additional form of protection. It did for my late wife, Inara. In the end, the choice is up to you."

Chapter 19

The choice is up to you.

A six-word sentence that most people find themselves contemplating an answer for at one point or another in their life, wouldn't you say? And Sable was most definitely left with a dilemma.

If you were in her position, what would you do? Would you allow the little voices in your ear, the shadows if you will, to convince you to do something that went against what you believed? That's what Sable was trying to determine for she didn't believe in taking a life at any stage, just as Eliza hadn't, but the fear of the unknown I'm sure was intense.

I cannot say this for certain, for there is nothing in what I found written on the subject, but I would imagine those blasted demonic pests were riding her hard at that moment - playing upon her worst fears. Seeping into her every being, trying to get her to rid the world of the children she'd conceived, because they most definitely, as Kalabernus had said, did not want them to be born.

And for a reason.

Would history repeat itself? Or would Sable be able to see past the fear and allow her heart to rule her head? Guess you'll have to wait and see.

- - -

Her mind racing with all she learned, Sable watched as Bastion quietly stood and left her alone in the living room. Thinking back over everything Kahner told her and her discussion with Bastion, she realized how anxious and worried they were over what her decision would be.

Unconsciously reaching up toward her chest, Sable grasped once again for the elk teeth she would normally have about her neck. Frustrated at its lack of presence, she allowed her gaze to shift about the room uneasily. She wondered whether the shadows were present now. Were they trying even as she sat there to probe into her mind and fill her with unnecessary fears and anxiety?

She couldn't lie. She was more than a little afraid. Being able to know Kahner's thoughts, had been more than a little disconcerting. To be able to do that throughout her entire pregnancy was an overwhelming notion. Covering a hand over her belly Sable grimaced. Three babies - each one with their own ability. Bearing and raising children was difficult enough but to have three; all of whom are gifted. How could she possibly do that? And even if she chose to carry and have them, would she want to be raising them alone?

Sable had become accustomed to Kahner's presence within her life in such a short time and had to admit she was having trouble imagining living without him. She wasn't sure what that meant yet, but she also didn't know if she was ready for what was to come.

Taking a deep breath Sable finally made at least one decision.

It was time for bed.

Placing the book on the coffee table she stood and put the fire out. Heading upstairs she walked quietly down the hallway, checking her children's bedrooms to make sure they were okay. Seeing they were all sleeping soundly, Sable smiled contentedly then stepped further down the hall. She hesitated only briefly outside the bedroom door, then turned the knob and opened it.

The room was dark, cast in shadows by the blinds covering the windows. Making her way around the bed she slid off her slippers and crawled into bed under the blankets, grateful for the feel of the plush mattress beneath her. Rolling to her side her gaze shifted to the pillow next to her.

Kahner stared back at her, his eyes wide as though having been awake the whole time.

"You're awake."

"You're here."

Silence surrounded them. Neither one moved or spoke.

"Kahner, I'm tired of running."

"So am I," he replied, glad to be home at last after nearly fifteen years.

"I don't want to be another Eliza," Sable choked out, her voice filling with raw emotion. She could hear the sharp inhale of breath and could see in his eyes the yearning he had for what she carried.

"Then don't be," Kahner said imploringly, for the first time allowing his tough guy façade to break. "Be my wife, Sable. Let me keep you and all our children safe. Allow me to show you how good marriage can be when two people love and care for each other. I'm not Lionel. I'd never hurt you as he did."

Sable closed her eyes on a wave of relief. She'd been so afraid his only reasons for marrying her were for protection and for wanting the babies.

"Oh, Honey. I want it all. I want all of you, regardless of what you carry," he insisted, clearly having gleaned her thoughts.

"Okay," she said softly.

Kahner tensed. "Is that a yes?"

"On one condition." Her eyes bore into his with an intense stare.

"Anything. You simply need to ask," he insisted urgently, wanting nothing more than to have the woman in his bed attached to his hip for life. Technically on paper, they were already married, though he wasn't sure Sable was aware of that yet. Unbeknownst to her, Bastion slipped a marriage license in with the other documents he had her sign earlier in the day for her new identity. His father claimed when Kahner confronted him on it that he had foreseen she would agree. But as they both knew, other people's decisions could change an outcome drastically, so his father's visions weren't necessarily predestined. Gazing into her sparkling amber eyes, he anxiously awaited her response, wondering what she would ask of him.

"Give me back my blasted necklace."

Kahner blinked.

He had not expected that.

With a straight face, he pushed up on the bed then leaned forward into her impudent stare. "And what do I get in return?" He grinned devilishly.

Snorting loudly Sable lay in the bed unyielding and unfazed by his question. She wasn't stupid. She knew full well what he had just been thinking and was beginning to rather like this new ability she was experiencing. Regardless of the ceremony held on Friday for show, she was aware that it was her wedding night. But only if she agreed.

Bastion had thought he'd been slick by slipping the marriage license in with the documents she signed. She'd known all along. The question had merely been whether she would follow through on her decision and ignore the fear - and the shadows - which plagued her. Lips pursing in an impish grin, Sable's eyes glimmered with mischief.

"Give it to me and you'll find out."

Brow quirking with interest Kahner deftly moved toward the bedside table and reached into the drawer. Pulling a small object out, he dangled it before her.

Sitting up, Sable grabbed for it.

"Ah, ah, ah," Kahner tisked playfully. "What do I get in return?"

Snatching it from his grasp Sable quickly shoved it over her head. Then she pounced, pinning him to the bed as she spoke seductively.

"Me."

Epilogue

What?

What are you looking here for?

You think there's something more?

Oh, right. I get it. You're looking here because I said you'd find out who I, Vortigern Black, am at the end of the RavenCroft story. Let me ask you something first. Have you figured it out yet?

I'm betting you haven't yet, right?

Well, here's the thing. I'm not going to tell you yet.

Now don't get mad.

I specifically said I'd tell you who I was at the end of the RavenCroft story. This book here is just the beginning of their tale for it only covered how it all got started. Kahner loved Eliza, lost his child, then met Kalysta. They came together, fell in lust, then in love, and, in the end, agreed to marry. I assure you it was a beautiful wedding ceremony too, even though it was small and held at the RavenCroft ranch in their living room. But the RavenCrofts story isn't over yet. As I said, it's just the beginning.

Tell you what, I will give you a hint, though. I am one of the people who were present at the ranch house when Sable found out she was pregnant. Does that help?

Hahaha.

Good luck figuring it out.

I'll catch you in the next one.

AUTHORS NOTE

Thank you for taking the time to read my story. I truly hope you enjoyed it. And if you wouldn't mind… Please be sure to leave a review of Terrible Karisma at amazon.com. I'd love to hear from you. And Thank you! I'd also like to welcome you to experience…

Kayos Effect
An Unfortunate Lineage
Volume II

OR, if you are disinclined toward reading faith-based fiction at this time, (and there is nothing wrong with that, of course) you may skip on to…

Karisma Trouble
An Unfortunate Lineage
Volume III

OR, if you're just plain bored with all of this, you think you've got all the answers, and have already figured out who Vortigern Black is then feel free to skip over everything and go straight to the finale.

Karisma Kayos: Out of Time
An Unfortunate Lineage Finale
Volume VII

On the other hand, what's wrong with getting all the facts first? Even the great Hercule Poirot of Agatha Christie was capable of being wrong. At least once. But only ever once. (Scratches head) Or at least I think it was only once, or was that…?

Oh, heck. (sighs) More research…

Delaine Christine

Character List Of Suspects

Vortigern Black - Narrator of the RavenCroft story and a character within. But which one of the following characters lays claim to the pseudonym?

Bastion RavenCroft - Patriarch of the RavenCroft clan and father of the following from eldest to youngest. Triplets: Kahner, Kalturek, Kalabernus. Fraternal twins: Drayke and Mackenzie. And finally, the baby of the family, Synedra.

Kahner RavenCroft - Firstborn of triplets, he is married to Eliza RavenCroft

Eliza RavenCroft - Wife of Kahner RavenCroft.

Kalturek RavenCroft - The Second-born of triplets, he is married to Stephanie RavenCroft.

Character List of Suspects

Stephanie RavenCroft - Wife of Kalturek RavenCroft, she desperately wants a gifted child

Kalabernus RavenCroft - Third born of triplets, he is single and a recluse because of his gift.

Drayke RavenCroft – Mackenzie's fraternal twin and fourth born, he is married to Laynie RavenCroft.

Laynie RavenCroft - Wife of Drayke RavenCroft, she also wants children, but it doesn't matter whether they are gifted or not.

Mackenzie Funnie (RavenCroft) – Drayke's fraternal twin and fifth born, she is married to Dr. S.T. Funnie.

Dr. S.T. Funnie - He is the husband of Mackenzie Funnie (RavenCroft).

Synedra Kayme (RavenCroft) - Sixth born and the baby of the family, she is married to Nathan Kayme.

Nathan Kayme - He is the husband of Synedra Kayme (RavenCroft), he is a private investigator.

Agent Ricardo Pegueros - He works for the Central Intelligence Agency (CIA) in undercover operations, specializing in information retrieval.

Kalysta Radford - Wife of Lionel Radford for over ten years, she is the mother of Lisa (10), and fraternal twins Adam (7), and Jordon Radford (7).

Lionel Radford - Younger brother to Kobi Radford, he and his brother are drug cartel kingpins with brutal tempers. Lionel is married to Kalysta Radford and is the father of Lisa (10), Adam (7), and Jordan Radford (7).

Kobi Radford - Older brother of Lionel Radford. He heads the drug cartel left to them by their father.

Author Delaine Christine

Who is she really? Take a guess from within
She can relate with her story my friend.
An author of fiction who writes what she knows
Could that mean she's a mother of three,
you suppose?

If you guessed, yes, then you would be right.
A daughter and twins, they're her greatest delight.
And though being gifted might sound really cool
Her only talent's bad poems, silly fool.

For more about the
An Unfortunate Lineage series
and the author

www.vortigernblack.com

https://www.smashwords.com/profile/view
/DelaineChristine

Or to Contact the Author:
delainechristine15@gmail.com